SHADOWQUEEN.
BLOOD MOON

MADELYNNE ELLIS

KELL'S PROPHECY

When the Blood Moon rises, the demons' prince will wake from his thousand-year slumber and cast a shadow across the sun. The city will become *youkai* paradise, a vast playground of perversity and vice. However, his rebirth will encompass many stages, during which time we will know him only by his mark."

1. HALL OF SHADOWS

**

"The Ti is unique to the individual, and is indestructible,
e'en after death it remains.
The Ti resides in the Death Ward,
where it ever hungers for the Ci'th of the living."
–The Book of Death, Lesson 12.

**

Blaze Makaresh mounted the dais with his eyes closed, only when he reached the top did he look down. They'd dressed her in red and black, in a gown cut narrow around the waist with a fairy tale skirt of gossamer layers and a huge train that spilled over the sides of the platform on which she lay. An outfit fit for a queen.

His queen.

In her hands she held clasped a single grey rose. Somehow they'd made her look perfect and whole. The neck of the dress reached high on her throat, disguising the wound he knew was there.

Impossible to believe she was gone. Wrong too that she hadn't died fighting. As a warrior that's the way it should have been. Death in battle, not subjected to the ignoble execution Talon had inflicted.

His gaze turned red at the thought of Talon, and the curtain behind him caught fire. The flames ripped through the fabric, leaving behind a ragged cobweb of ash and the smell of burnt cotton.

Get a grip, Blaze.

Then again, why should he? Who friggin' cared about the damned tapestry? Not him. He didn't care about the palace or the moon or any of the youkai who lurked in the shadows, keeping well out of his way, but who remained ever present. He knew he tried their patience, but they could wait forever. He had no reason to leave this room, no reason to fight at all anymore.

"Asha." There was no heat in her skin as he curved his palm to her pale cheek, only a waxy cold that penetrated right to his bones. The chill of death, he sensed its pull, the silent, blessed lure of the grave.

Die and be with her.

He could do it. End it all here and now.

Only... No, that wasn't what he desired. He wanted life, living, breathing life with her, not to spend an eternity decaying in one another's arms.

"This wasn't what I intended." He voice echoed in the vast chamber, and seem to mock him. The fact was that he ought never to have let her go. The memory of their final kiss—hastily stolen before he crossed the Division Bridge—replayed ad nauseam in his thoughts. He should have run after her—done something.

He bent, brushed his lips against her cold brow.

They should never have met. She ought to have left him behind. He'd been nothing but a weight upon her back, while she'd given him everything. Her time, her loyalty and protection, her heart and—a sob erupted from his throat—her life.

Tears dripped off the end of his nose and wet her skin as he kissed her face. The scent of roses filled his nostrils and became overpowering, leaving him nauseous. The taste of death filled his mouth. Another fire started across the room, this time a tablemat, and then a dish of potpourri. Like anyone would miss that. What the fuck use was it anyway? Slivers of bark and seed pods mixed with glitter and a dowsed in patent 'old lady' scent, that horrid mix of lavender, patchouli and cat's piss, with a hint of sour cream and thread of nicotine.

The smell of it burning didn't make it any more palatable, but nor could he tear himself from Asha's side to find anything with which to dampen the flames.

Blaze rested his head against her breast. The stillness, the lack of a gentle thud in his ear rent another tear in his tough guy façade. He'd been working hard on it too, since he arrived here. When you chose to hang out with demons, hell, it was important to try and look the part. Someone had stripped the leathers from his back. He didn't recall who. Maybe they'd burned away. Except the flames hadn't bothered to clothe him again, that had been a person. They'd dressed him in princely black and gold, in material so supple it felt like his own skin.

If only his own skin wasn't so tight.

"Asha," he whispered again. Her name formed a constant echo in his mind. He needed her. He couldn't let her go. Wasn't ready to. He could still feel her inside of him.

Wasn't that the point?

Burning inside him.

Feeding him.

Lending him strength.

"What strength?" He had no strength. He had nothing without her.

Blaze buried his face in her hair, seeking the memory of her in the form of her scent. Eyes closed, he could almost... almost believe. No, it was gone, the pungent aroma of burning potpourri drowning out everything else. Frantic now, panic welling inside him, Blaze clutched her to his chest.

Talon—he was going to bloody kill him. Slow roast the bastard, and extract every snowy feather from his wings one by one.

But he couldn't leave her... He couldn't let go.

"SMELLS LIKE A harpy's armpit. What the fuck's he doing in there?"

"Grieving." Raven inched back behind the fretwork colonnade that separated the Hall of Shadows from the gallery that overlooked the Queen's Gardens, to find Florian stooped a few feet away, his eye pressed to a gap within the brass screen.

"It's to be expected. Flo, he's in a waking dream, replaying events." Blaze had been in there from the moment he woke. They'd had to knock him out on the return journey from the warehouse to stop him torching everything in sight. He'd become a walking inferno since completing the triumvirate. Although at present, he was more like a hot water cannon.

"Her passing is hardly a great loss."

"Flo." Raven shot a warning at the other guy, but as normal it failed to make an impact. Stupid fool had always possessed about as much empathy as a shoelace, except for where his sister was concerned.

"What? I'm just saying what we're all thinking. She's been butchering us for years. You're not telling me you'd accepted her. She was never going to be his queen. It was all talk, Raven, a whole heap of bullshit to get him to act."

There was no denying there'd been a liberal sprinkling of deceit in some of what had been said to motivate Blaze into action, but, "It wasn't all talk, and for one of Talon's marionettes, she wasn't all that bad."

Florian turned his back to the fretwork and dug a paper bag from his pocket. "Sounds like she did a number on you. I heard she powdered your brother. Want one?" He waved the bag in Raven's direction, while simultaneously pulling out part of its contents.

Raven pushed the offered dainties away, unsure whether they were strawberry laces or rat intestines. Asha hadn't killed his brother, Talon had. Nor had Asha wheedled her way into his affections... Nah, his shell was far tougher than that. She was still one of them. But they'd understood one another, two warriors, thrown together and given a common cause. He'd respected her, and she'd loved Blaze. There was no getting around that. She'd protected his prince when he hadn't been around to do his job. He owed her for that.

Fact was, without her, they'd all be stuffed. Blaze needed her. Without her he was incomplete. Her life force had turned him from a pawn into a king. It was just a shame she'd had to die to make it work.

"Think he'll want one?" The bag rustled as Florian held it outstretched again. He took a step beyond the screen heading towards Blaze before Raven dragged him back into the shadows.

"I know it's hard, but try not to get yourself roasted."

Stupid, dumb bastard.

A malicious smile spread across Florian's over-generous mouth. "Aw, you're taking my hide into account. I'm overwhelmed. I never knew you cared."

Raven shrugged off his hold, and tried to ignore the kiss Florian blew him. No point in giving the irritating bastard a rise.

"Face it, big guy. I'm only doing what you daren't. We can't leave him there wallowing, because we can't do squat without him. I'm prepared to sacrifice a few hair follicles to the cause. How about you?"

Raven slowly uncurled his fists. It didn't matter what anyone said. Blaze wasn't going anywhere until he'd worked a few things out of his system and got himself well and truly worked up for some revenge. Until then, the entire human population of the City could come knocking on the door and it still wouldn't shift him.

As for the hair follicles... Florian hadn't been in that burning warehouse. He hadn't seen the fireball Blaze had created with his thoughts. Those that had were still talking in husky voices and soothing their burns. Raven still had two enormous hand-shaped blisters on his chest. They were healing, but slowly. There'd been neither time nor opportunity to do anything to speed up the process since they arrived back. His first priority had been tending Blaze, and then there'd been Asha to lay out.

"He has to get over it."

"You just don't get it, do you?" Raven wrenched at his topknot, causing the leather thong that held it in place to snap, so that he then had to refasten it.

"All I'm saying... Hasn't the guy heard of revenge, retribution? This is the start. It's how it's meant to be. It's a reason to fight. Isn't that what he wanted?"

Admittedly, Blaze had questioned his involvement. He didn't see himself as their ruler. He feared the destruction of the town below, feared the changes their presence there would bring.

"Nowhere is it written that our rule on Earth comes about from the Prince going psycho after his consort's head is sliced off." Raven snarled.

"It might not be written but that doesn't mean it ain't fact. The history books can be amended later. Right now, we need him on his feet and functioning. It's not as if he's been an overly active figure so far. It's time we roused him, and dealt with this sulk."

Raven rubbed his hand across his mouth. Fact

was he'd dearly like to slam Florian into next week. Okay, so maybe they did need Blaze pronto. No point in imagining Talon had gone home to sit idly in some rocking chair ready for them to make a first move, but...

"You know Florian's right." Skaa slid out of an alcove to join them, accepting one of Florian's snacks, which he sucked down in one great pull.

Great, just what the buffoon needed—back up. And dangerous back up at that.

"We don't have time for his grief. The Blood Moon is out there. You can be sure Talon's not sitting idle watching clouds pass across its surface."

Damn. There was no need for Skaa to go echoing his thoughts.

"If Talon has any sense he's manning a fire hose." Sorrow flew in from the twilight sky. He landed straddling the balcony, and gave the scene beyond the fretwork a long hard look. "Bit obsessive, that boy. It's not healthy."

"Let's stick to the fire hoses," Raven remarked. "Tell me about those. You've been out over the City, I take it."

"Only for a very short jaunt. I thought it prudent to follow up on what impact Talon's actions had back home."

"And?"

Sorrow shook his head. "If there's uproar, it's damned quiet uproar. The populace are more concerned with saving their houses than us up here. The wind's carried the flames westward down through the Birdcage. Another few hours at its current pace and it'll be licking up the side of the Eyrie, maybe even threatening the cathedral."

"That should keep him busy."

All three of his companions shook their heads.

"Talon's not going to sit around. He's out for a crown. Rest assured he's doing everything he can to make sure he gets it. He's missed two opportunities now to remove Blaze from the game, you can be damn sure he's not going to fail a third."

"Two?" Florian asked. "At the meeting, and..."

"He had him caged at the cathedral for a while before Asha freed him. And but for a moment's distraction, he'd have taken Blaze's head along with hers."

"Still, he can't reach him in here."

"Can't he?" Skaa remarked darkly. "Are we all so sure about that?"

Raven turned his back on them. It didn't matter how much finger waggling they all did, Blaze was non-functioning, as distant to them now as he'd been the last fifty years. There'd be no persuading or cajoling him into action. He was lost, knotted up in his grief, and only time would change that.

Sorrow came up beside him, stroked his fingers through the wisps of hair at the base of Raven's neck that had worked loose from his topknot. "We're not trying to be insensitive, just stating the facts. Now isn't the time to wallow. We have to act. So, tell us what it's going to take."

"A miracle." Nothing short of that.

2. CAPTIVE

"Green eyes and green teeth."
- I Spy a Demon by Izumo.

"I WANT TO see her," Jaku insisted.

The demon stood on the other side of the bars, arms folded, his razor sharp teeth locked in an angry smile. He hadn't twitched so much as an eyelid in over an hour, even when Jaku had kicked over the glorious china pisspot they'd left him.

They'd locked him in a cage. No magical bars on this one, nothing as elaborate as the device Talon had used to contain Blaze. Nope, just plain old-fashioned steel. He had a cot, a broken chamber pot and nothing else. They'd removed all the interesting accessories normally secreted about his person, including the buttons of his coat. Fools obviously didn't think the pottery was worthy of concern or they'd never have allowed him it. Demons had thick hides, but even they had weak points, and the china shards were enough to shred a vein or two, maybe even take out an eye.

Jaku lay on the floor. He'd rolled off the cot

the moment he woke, memories of Talon's betrayal sharp in his mind. He wanted to know what had happened, and how he'd come to be here. Presumably the youkai had carried him here from the warehouse. They ought to have let him burn. It would have been a fitting end. He deserved to die, just as he deserved the pain that scourged his fingers. He knew there'd been a fire, the scent of smoke clung to his clothing and hair, and the skin on the left side of his face felt unnaturally wrinkled and tight. There wasn't a mirror to reflect the damage done to his face, but he knew from what he could see of his hands that the result wouldn't be pretty.

"I want to see Asha." Somehow he knew the youkai had won, that they had her here. It made sense. If they'd lost, he wouldn't be a prisoner. Not that he'd ever support Talon again. That relationship was finally over.

Rigidly stoic, the guard ignored the demand, but soon after the cell door opened and another demon came in. He set down a small three-legged stool and hunched onto its surface. "You were her partner, were you not, Jaku?"

This was one of the three who'd attended the meeting with Blaze. Through his horribly dry eyes, Jaku studied the demon's profile; handsome in the sense that women liked, big jaw, big shoulders, with features both neat and regular. Only the eyes were weird, mismatched, the right oddly dilated.

"Who are you? Why did you bring me here? Why not just leave me to die?"

The demon tapped his long agile fingers to his

lips. "I'm Raven Idriss, as for your other questions. I'm sure you can answer those for yourself."

"You think I'll be of use to you," he replied slowly, Talon's image looming large in his thoughts. So the deranged bastard had escaped the warehouse. That fact didn't surprise him. Talon always had a trick or five up his sleeves. He wasn't sure the mad alchemist actually recalled how to die. But then, his apparent invulnerability had been a large part of his appeal. Who didn't pray for a little of that—a little protection?

"Talk to me, Jaku. I can help with revenge."

Quietly he began to laugh. "Do you really think that because Talon deceived me, we're suddenly on the same side? I won't help you. I'll never help you." He turned his back, and slipped a triangular shard of broken pottery from his sleeve. Scum. Liars. Monsters. He turned the shard in his hand. He'd hunted youkai all his adult life, seen the impact they had on people's lives, watched countless downward spirals. It always ended the same way, with heart ache and death.

Take a demon lover and you wound up dead.

Asha had been an addict. It seemed inevitable looking back that she'd eventually fall for their tricks and become hooked upon their poisons. He ought to have severed the link between her and Blaze the moment of its inception. But he'd been soft. He'd been taken in by a pretty face. He had only to look around to see where that had got him—pounded like an animal. And Asha? Hell knows where her mind was trapped. She'd been little more than an animated corpse in the warehouse, Blaze having sucked the vitality off her bones.

Damn fool that he was, he'd trusted Talon to make things right, instead Talon had used her, same as he'd been using her for years.

"Where's Asha? I want to see her." He tried to temper the anger in his voice, but the request still emerged as a growl.

"Unfortunately that's not possible. Did you know Talon had wings?"

Jaku clamped his lips together. He didn't want to think about Talon, and the vast array of mistakes he'd made. And he certainly wasn't discussing revenge with a demon. Although—wings! Talon had exposed himself. It seemed things had got rather interesting at that meeting. Had Ouran and Kairn survived the encounter? Perhaps they were prisoners, too. Talon wouldn't like the knowledge that he was a demon leaking out.

"Judging by your silence, you knew. You realised he was one of us, and yet you still followed him. Ironic, don't you think? The Talon, raised as an army to slaughter the evil youkai, and yet you're led by one."

"There's no irony involved. He isn't youkai anymore than Asha is. Talon's simply been infected with youkai blood. He's not a demon, he's something else."

Raven released a throaty laugh. "He's something else all right. I won't argue with you over that." He leaned forward a little and planted both palms upon his knees, the reflection of his form visible in the bars. "She's dead, Jaku. I can't take you to her, because Talon ended it. He severed her head."

Jaku up and turned while his mind was still

screaming, "What!" and aimed straight for the demon's eye, but didn't quite make it before the son of a bitch reacted. The china triangle scored along Raven's cheekbone instead, leaving behind a weeping red line. Jaku reversed his stroke and ran another cut across the demon's throat.

He kept at it, striking hard and fast and always at a different target, meanwhile ignoring the tightening pain in his chest.

"Enough!" The fist connected first with his temple and then right between the eyes, setting off a series of explosions, first in his nose, and then looping around through his jaw to leave his ears ringing. The demon had a punch on him like a battering ram.

"Ruddy fucking Talon, you're all so damned cocky. Think you can take out anyone." The iron fist sideswiped him, leaving Jaku sprawled over the cot, gazing up at the opaque metal ceiling. "You're in a cage. Even if you drop me no one's going to ring a bell and call timeout. Believe me, I'm the only ally you've got. So, chill the fuck out."

Raven wiped away the blood from his throat and peered in disgust at the smears across his fingers, then face set in a no nonsense frown extended his other hand towards Jaku. "Get up."

Get up! Jaku swung up again, both fists clamped around the improvised dagger. He feigned right then ducked low this time aiming for the thick arteries at the top of the leg which fed the groin. Score one. The shard pierced the leather and stuck in the wound, provoking a bellow of outrage. Demon claws sliced open his back looking for a purchase and somehow thrust him forward using Jaku's already forward momentum to send him between Raven's legs and head first into the bars.

The guard leered at him from outside the cage, ghoulishly slobbering with its tongue hanging out. It didn't offer to assist, but looked likely to pounce once there was an easy meal lain out.

He wasn't becoming any demon's dinner.

Jaku rolled, only for Raven to drop right on top of him.

Up close the demon smelled of sex. The coppery tang of its spilled blood hung in the air, whetting his palate, and causing sparks wherever it hit a nerve-ending on his tongue or in his nose. Shit! He'd known people get high on a teaspoon of their dust but he'd never known you could get tingly from simply inhaling the buggers.

With those weirdly mismatched eyes Raven stared down at him, their noses mere inches apart. The heart of the right eye, where there should have been a pupil, glowed like a hurricane lantern. Beside it, the left seemed a barren wasteland of ash. Trapped by the intense glare, Jaku remained rigid as Raven tilted his head and sniffed the side of his neck. He tried to numb the insistent throb of his body reacting to the youkai poison by thinking of all the horrors he'd witnessed at their hands, but the memories didn't quell the sense of excitement or the erotic tingle that drip-fed all his pleasure centres.

"Get off me," he groaned, his protest sounded particularly feeble.

A warm wet tongue licked over his pulse point in response.

"I'm not sure... There's something..." Raven

shook his head and the light in his right eye went out, leaving the iris a frosted-lilac colour. "Are you cool now?" He took some of his weight onto his hands and knees, allowing Jaku to suck down a welcome breath of relief.

They were still too close; Jaku's arms still pinned, but some of the fight had seeped away as the erotic buzz had grown. Now he looked into Raven's eyes and wondered what the hell had happened.

"How did she die? A fight?" Considering how volatile the players at that meeting were, it was hardly a surprise to find something had caused them to erupt.

"No fight. Just cold cruel murder."

Raven lifted off Jaku, and settled back on his stool. "Talon's intention, at least what he claimed, was to sever the link between her and Blaze."

Jaku's anger at the youkai came flooding back, but he restricted his reaction to a clenching of his fists. He wanted to hear what the demon had to say, and that meant staying put. He pushed up a little onto his elbows.

The shard he'd planted in Raven's thigh remained in the wound, although a Blood Rain crust now surrounded it. His interest prompted Raven to pull it loose. He threw the chip beyond the bars and clamped a hand over the wound. Jaku cast a speculative glance at the remains of the chamber pot that still littered the cell floor. Listening was good, but so was having a back-up plan.

Raven lifted his hand from the wound upon his thigh and took a peek. "Touch another of those shards and I'll make you my next meal."

Jaku curled his extended fingers into a fist again. *Okay, time to just listen up.* Demon was staring at him oddly again, like there was something about him he couldn't quite figure.

"So Talon killed her. Blaze was doing that anyway."

"No, he was determined to keep her alive."

"She was a mess, out of her mind. Blaze had already destroyed her by feeding off her soul."

Raven's eyebrows shot up. He rubbed at his chin before replying. "Blaze didn't steal anything from her. He'd bonded with her. Accidentally, admittedly, but it was never his intention to endanger her. Talon severed her grip on life, not Blaze. He had no plan to ever do that. It's what we all wanted, for him to use the power he gained from the bond to ascertain our victory and place us in ascendancy, but he wouldn't complete the triumvirate, because he knew she wouldn't survive."

All very enlightening, but he wasn't sure why the demon was telling him. Jaku shrugged off the odd prickly premonition running through the back of his neck. Bastard demon knew something he didn't, and was probably trying to goad him into doing or revealing something. "Do you see the future with that eye of yours?" What sense was there in hiding the fact that he'd figured it out?

"No. I see truths. But like anything, they are only snapshots. There's rarely any context to place them in."

"And you saw something when you looked at me just now?"

"Yes."

"What? What did you see?"

Raven shook his head, the barest hint of a smile gracing his beautifully expressive lips. "I'm not sure yet. Maybe I'll let you know when I work it out." He rose, and folded up the stool. "I'll come back later."

"No, wait!" Jaku pushed up onto his feet. "Tell me what happened. Talon escaped, but what of my companions? What happened to Asha's remains?" If Blaze cared so very much for her as this demon seemed to suggest, surely he'd brought her here with him, to wherever here was—presumably their upside down castle in the sky.

"If she's here, I want the chance to say goodbye. I promised her that."

Long ago, they'd sworn an oath to each other that when the end finally came they'd see the other properly entombed and settled in eternal peace. Leastways... Well, he'd never been entirely honest over that. He'd failed his family once. When he died, he intended to finally put things right. He'd stand guardian outside their crypt, but Asha claimed she'd spent enough time running from the Ghost Wind to ever want to be part of it.

Hand upon the lock, Raven paused. "She's laid out as befits a queen. You can't go to her. Blaze is with her, and he's out of his mind with grief. As for your friends, I've no idea whether they survived or not. They were of little concern."

Blaze's grief sounded real. Whereas any remorse Talon might be showing would be an outright lie. Jaku shook his head. He was still crazy dumb if he expected to hear the truth from the youkai, even if he couldn't find much fault in this one, beyond simple genetics.

Maybe he'd misjudged.

Raven swung open the cage door and stepped outside. He locked up again and handed the key to the guard.

"Wait, please," Jaku beseeched him. "If you won't let me see her, then at least call Vervain. I know you've met him. He helped you before. He can help you again. Let him tend her. Don't let the Ghost King claim her."

3. LOST SOULS

******
"The Ci'th is the animating force.
It is the difference between life and death,
and is the energy source upon which we all thrive."
–The Book of Death, Lesson 13.
******

AWARENESS RIPPLED OVER Blaze's skin like icy water. He lay upon the dais alongside Asha, his body pressed fast to hers, her frozen fingers clasped tight within his palm. Sometimes he imagined he felt the rise and fall of her chest.

Raven wouldn't come here, which meant one of the others. He raised his head from her breast. How dare they intrude here? Surely they realised he had no time for their petty concerns.

Two of them emerged together from beyond the latticework screening at the far end of the room. Blaze watched them approach through narrowed eyes. Grace, Florian, siblings too stupid to comprehend the complexities of grief. *Whatever it is, however important you think it. Leave now.*

He didn't speak a single word aloud, but he knew they heard him, and the emotion he sent alongside the thoughts resonated off the walls. But like he said, too stupid.

"Time to leave the dead meat behind before Talon comes chomping at our arses," Florian remarked, one foot raised to mount the platform on which the dais sat.

For a moment, Blaze was so stunned by the total insensitivity of the prick that he gaped in disbelief.

As for Grace, he knew why Grace had come. Even now, while cowering behind her brother's back she was eyeing him like he was a frozen dessert, forked tongue sliding back and forth over her dry lips. Hope had never left her, and with his chosen queen gone, why shouldn't she step into the void, take up the position she'd envisioned for herself all along. She couldn't see he had no desire, no respect for her person, that he couldn't comprehend even the future possibility of being with another. Ever.

"Get out," he insisted, but without raising his voice.

"What sort of prissy, gutless prince are you?" Florian continued, drawing his fingers through the strands of his luxurious mane of hair. "We're on the cusp, and you're too busy weeping to take action. We need a prince who can lead us. One who has the strength to stand tall and bring death to the Talon and their supporters. Crying over her won't bring her back. If she means so very much, then consume her and be done, but move on. We need to act now, ahead of the storm."

He needed to act. Oh, yes! He needed to rid himself of impertinent intruders.

A sharp tingly sensation flooded Blaze's sinuses and filtered down to the end of his nose. His eyes closed with the pain of it. It felt like someone had shoved a crocheting hook up his nose and was wiggling it about inside his brain, but even as the pain spiked and gave way to tears, his internal focus never wavered.

Shut them up. Make them understand the bond he'd formed. How he had a piece of Asha locked away inside himself, but what he wanted was a whole, living, breathing person, one who was flawed and unpredictable, but who always had his best interests at heart. A woman he loved. How dearly he wanted to say that to her face and see the understanding light up the depths of her eyes.

All that taken away and smashed because of an age old prophecy he'd somehow stumbled upon.

The sound of gristly meat being shred from bones drowned out the accompanying screams. When he cleared the water from his eyes, it was to find the pair of them had been folded into one. Neither male nor female, the new entity screamed in rage and then collapsed. Blaze left Asha's side and hauled it by the ankle to the edge of the room. At least now, he and Asha could be alone again, and maybe they, whatever they had become, would fully comprehend. Synergy, symbiosis, the bond he'd formed wasn't a human marriage that could be dissolved on a whim. Asha and he, they were eternal.

RAVEN WALKED OUT of the prison cell and kept on working his way up from the bowels of the castle until he couldn't climb any further. Having bypassed the Hall of Shadows without even peeking at Blaze, he finally settled on the roof, or at least the curious little cap house above the stairs. Glassless windows opened from the tiny stone room onto the magenta sky where the full moon hung, now covered with a rosy blush. The hue had deepened since he'd last looked, so that it more closely resembled the colour of blood.

They needed a miracle.

He rested his elbows on one of the window apertures and looked down, avoiding the view of the City. Not that much was visible through the swollen cloud of smoke and ash.

He'd found their miracle. He just didn't trust it.

Bad thing his eyesight. It hurt like hell to see into a person and know their fate was already written. Not that he generally concerned himself with human affairs. Jaku's ghosts were already eating him alive, his actions would make no differences to that. Only Jaku could change his own fate.

"Raven?" Sorrow appeared in the doorway, his face flushed from having run up the stairs. "I think you'd better come down."

"What's happened?"

"It's Blaze."

Of course it was.

"He's done... Well, he's done something to..." Sorrow licked his seemingly blistered lips. "I think you'd better see for yourself."

"WHAT HAPPENED?" Raven asked, as he pushed his way into the assembled group lurking behind the latticework screen that bordered the Hall of Shadows once again. "Didn't I tell you all to leave him alone? Did someone get fried?" If they had, they'd deserved it.

The bodies slowly stepped aside, providing him with a clear passage to the focus of their attention. Not, to his surprise, a cindered ruin, nor in fact any being he recognised. "What the fuck is that?" he asked Skaa who knelt by the... Actually, he didn't know what to call it.

Skaa rolled whatever it was over, prompting a groan that at least proved it was still breathing. "This, I think you'll find is a Florace."

Floris? "A what?" And then he saw it, as clearly as if he'd sewn them together himself. This was Grace and Florian, melted down and reformed anew as one being. The skin, still baby soft and raw, continued to knit over newly formed muscles and fused bones even as he watched. The wings, they were Grace's, as were the diamond pattern marking beginning to show across the buttocks and thighs, and in patches across the torso and beneath the arms, but the construction of the face, that was almost entirely Flo.

Almost, except for the fact that this thing had an additional set of eyes and barely any nostrils to speak of.

"Shit!" Nothing more eloquent would cut it. "Shit!" He cussed again for good measure. Okay, they needed Blaze back with them and sane. Never mind the Talon threat and the Blood Moon whose ruddy glow even now cast its shadow over the floor and walls. They needed Blaze well enough to undo whatever the hell he'd just done.

"What do we do?" Sorrow asked.

"Find it a bed, and post a guard. Nobody else go in to see Blaze."

"We need—" Skaa protested.

"We need to leave him alone. Give me a chance, okay?" He soothed them all into submission.

"Did you have any luck with the prisoner?" Sorrow asked once everyone else had left.

He shook his head. "Not exactly. Just an image. That's all."

"Is that why you were at the top of that bloody tower?"

"What was it?"

He shook his head. The man's fate wasn't in his hands. None of the real decisions involved were his to make. All he was doing was paving the way, and then he was only doing what he'd been asked.

Truth—not a course of action, was what he'd seen when he'd stared into Jaku's eyes.

"Are you up to another jaunt to the City, Sorrow?" he asked after a moment.

His subordinate removed his spectacles and placed them safely in a pocket. "What do you want from there?"

"I need you to bring me someone. A man who knew Asha."

"A man."

"His name is Vervain. If you hammer on the Lich Gate, I'm pretty certain he'll answer."

"If I explain what has happened, why would he come, or am I expected to snatch him?"

"You won't need to tell him anything. He'll already know what has happened to Asha. He's a Copse Man. He tends the dead. However, you might mention Jaku if he hesitates over accepting my invitation."

Sorrow bowed. "I'll do it, but I'm not sure I like the idea of involving bleeders in our affairs."

"My friend, they're already irrevocably entangled in them." He patted Sorrow on the shoulder. "Go now. Be quick and bring him here."

4. THE CI'TH AND THE M

J AKU STOOD UP from his cot the moment Raven appeared in the room. He watched the youkai cross the bare chamber and instruct the guard to open the cage. Raven stood in the opened doorway, not crossing the threshold of bars.

"Here," he flipped something in the air towards Jaku. "It might help."

Jaku caught the pot with his bad hand. Muscle memory took time to eradicate. Throw something and his hand shot out to catch it, didn't matter that the impact of the pot set squibs off between his fingertips and his brain. The strange brackish goop inside the pot smelled vaguely familiar, some alchemical formula intended to heal. Paraffin based, maybe. It might take some of the sting out of his wounds, but it wouldn't alleviate the discomfort in his heart. He'd screwed up again. Him, his misplaced loyalty and his dubious actions, they'd heralded Asha's death. He'd trusted Talon when he already knew better, but it had been easy to fool himself into thinking he was keeping an open mind when really he'd shoved his head right up his own arse.

Asha had been right all along. She'd seen through the lies, and helped Blaze, disregarding years of Talon indoctrination. Blaze was the instrument of change. Talon—a traitor, a liar, and a fraud. The list of epithets went on indefinitely, but none of them choked him so much as the notion that this was all his fault. If he'd thought for even a moment, he'd have seen what was coming.

"Is Blaze still with her? Can I see her now?"

Raven shook his head. The lines that suddenly furrowed his brow and made his cheekbones stand proud instantly quelled Jaku's urge to demand why. Something had happened. Something had changed since the demon's last visit.

"Blaze is still with her. He won't tolerate an intrusion."

Best response he could think to that was to nod, and settle down with the paraffin-scented gunge. Having scooped out a couple of fingers worth, Jaku set to work smoothing it over the burns on his face and hands. Touching them stung, but the gunge took much of the heat away. Actually, maybe it worked a little too well. Cold numbness spread through his cheek, forcing him to work his jaw to stop it freezing up. He ought to have realised that the medicine was demon strength.

"You said earlier that Blaze wasn't just

siphoning her energy, but that he'd formed a bond with her, what did you mean?"

Raven eyed him cautiously. 'They were soul mates. He'd begun the process of claiming her as his mate—his queen."

That explained why she was laid out in state.

"It must have smarted, the notion of her becoming your ruler, considering how many of you she'd killed."

"She didn't win the popular vote, but we're not a democracy. It was Blaze's choice, and we adhere to his wishes. Nor does it matter now. The important point is that the triumvirate is complete thanks to Talon's intervention. It would never have been otherwise. Blaze knew it would kill her. No human can survive with only one soul intact."

"So they're married in death." Jaku gave a low hacking laugh. It sounded like something out of a fairy tale, but then he'd spent all his adult life chasing fairy tales and trying to chop them into itty bitty pieces. It seemed a fitting end to her, somehow, and better than being incarcerated.

"No so, demon."

Both Jaku and Raven turned sharply, at the sound of the eavesdroppers approach. A shadowy figure emerged from the dark around the room's perimeter, causing the guard to come to attention, claws extended.

"Stand down," Raven barked. "I invited him here."

"Vervain?" Jaku enquired, recognising the grey woven fabric of the Death Warden's robe. Raven had understood, and done as he'd asked. He hadn't expected Vervain to come here though.

"Jaku." Vervain inclined his head, although only the tip of his nose was visible beneath the folds of his hood. He turned his head towards Raven and unfolded his arms. "You're mistaken, demon. There are ways in which a human can survive with only one soul, but they are not states we aspire to. As a matter of fact we hunt those of that ilk in much the same way that we hunt you, because they prey upon us much like you."

Raven turned sharply, leaving Jaku an escape route out of the cage if he chose to take it. The problem was, like Raven, he was too intrigued by Vervain's words.

"Explain," Raven demanded.

"How do the youkai accomplish it?" Vervain countered. He threw back the hood of his long robe, so that the lighting around the cage shone on the top of his bare scalp.

"With the triumvirate. We bind ourselves to a soul mate, but that practice has never been human practice. It's rare now even amongst my kind." He smiled, but as the emotion never reached his eyes, the result was more of a sneer. "We're too jealous of what power remains to us to risk sharing it anymore. The practice harkens back to our feudal days. But it's essential for our Prince to come into his true power."

Vervain warded off his words. "It's the details of the bond that interest me, not the politics. I understand that demons who form such a bond share the Ci'th between them, is that correct?"

Raven warily inclined his head. "The bond allows for the flow of Ci'th energy between the two partners, although it's commonly said that the male takes the soul into his keeping."

Which meant, "Blaze now holds what was Asha's Ci'th," Jaku blurted. Normally upon death the life essence was entirely lost, but Blaze still held onto hers.

"Precisely." Vervain nodded. "The youkai prince always forms a triumvirate. It's the power that he derives from it that keeps him on the throne. It's the reason why the youkai queen is known as the Shadow Queen. You remember that bit of your indoctrination, don't you Jaku?"

"Ti-consort," Raven corrected. "But what relevance is this? You may be unusual, human, but you're not invulnerable. I brought you here only because Jaku asked that I protect Asha from the Ghost King, and I know little of your dead and funereal rites. Why are we discussing the Ti and the Ci'th? Few of your kind even acknowledge that a person possesses two souls."

Vervain gave a patient nod. "The Ti soul is the personality, that which makes a person unique, and the Ci'th the animating force, the difference, at least for humans between life and death. It's one of the first lessons we learn when we become novices. Contrary to popular opinion the primary duty of the copse men is not to administer funereal rites, but to tend the Ti spirits in their houses and make sure the Ghost Wind doesn't grow so strong it overwhelms the living."

"The Ghost Wind is formed of those of us who aren't properly tended on our death," Jaku added.

Raven appeared intrigued, but his interest rapidly wavered and gave way to pacing.

"This is all very interesting but doesn't change the fact that Asha is dead. Talon severed her head."

"That is true, but Blaze holds her soul."

"And no human can survive with only one soul, or are you now claiming these ghosts, these Ti-spirits you tend are alive?"

"They are dead, but hunger. All that separates them from the living is the presence of the Ci'th. Who knows where it goes when we die, but in Asha's case, the Ci'th is intact. Blaze holds it. He need only reunite the parts."

"And she'll live," Jaku gasped. It hardly seemed possible and yet his heart thudded so much the surge of oxygen to his brain made him feel light-headed.

Raven seemed rather more cautious of the whole proposal. "I won't allow him to sever the triumvirate, not even to bring her back."

"That won't be necessary, in fact the triumvirate is the only reason this is possible. Normally those who defeat death do so by consuming the Ci'th of another at the point of death. Blaze need only feed her what is already hers by right."

"Feed?"

"The life essences of which the Ci'th is formed."

The same essences Talon had once stolen from Blaze—blood, tears and semen. All in a day's work for a demon.

"All you need do is find her Ti-spirit."

"And where might I find that?"

Vervain refolded his arms within his voluminous sleeves. "I think you know."

Raven scowled so that his brows drew low over his mismatched eyes. "You would have me enter the Death Ward while the Ghost Wind blows. Perhaps I was mistaken, and you're Talon's ally after all."

"I offer facts, nothing more. What you choose to do with them, demon, is entirely up to you."

The blowtorch lilac flare lit in Raven's strange eye, he stared long at Jaku, before finally turning away. "It seems preparations are required to parley with the dead."

5. PENANGGALAN

THE WIND'S LOW moan heralded their arrival at the crossroads. Raven braced himself and stood firm before the Lich Gate, placing faith in Vervain's ability to keep them safe. He hadn't any reason not to trust the copse-man, but one could never be too cautious, and standing at the crossroads at night, you had to be prepared to face the full brunt of the Ghost Wind.

Raven unintentionally tensed as Vervain hammered on the enormous gate and after a moment it swung inwards on silent hinges. All remained deathly quiet. Raven waited, body braced for impact, but nothing happened, and after a moment his shoulders sagged. Then just as he uncurled his toes ready to take a step forward, a swirling torrent of ice gushed over them. Hail stones smote his flesh, leaving bruises despite his clothing. Visibility fell to almost zero, just blurs of grey amongst the white. His eyes streamed, only for the tears to freeze upon his cheeks. Worse than the razor sharp shards were the voices, broken, discordant echoes of what had once been. Their very brittleness cut jagged lines across his souls.

Then just as abruptly the wind died and visibility was restored. Frost like sugar paste spilled over the crossroads and the crackle of frozen footsteps quickly approaching set his shoulders back up around his ears. Raven clutched tight the hilt of his sword. Wan faces leered out of the gloom. They rushed up close. Expecting the deathly chill of their touch, he was both surprised and relieved when instead they stopped short, forming instead a bubble around them.

"Vervain... Vervain..." Their hollow voiced moans of outrage and denial echoed off the steep sides of the nearby buildings. They swirled around the copse-man, drawn like moths to a beacon. One or two climbed into the weft of Vervain's robe, so that their shadows shifted across the silver-grey fabric before dissolving into the thread.

That the copse-man wielded such power over them came as a mild shock. The youkai had never had much cause for dealings with the wardens of the human dead, and hence they knew little of one another. One thing seemed clear enough, though. While in Vervain's company they would be fine here. Alone, they'd meet the same fate as the poor soul he'd witnessed in the clanking gibbets not so very long ago. Only bones lay there now, stripped clean of flesh.

Not that they were being left entirely unassaulted. He sensed the spirits teeth scraping along the outer edge of his aura, stealing tiny slivers of energy. One long fingered hand poked at his clothing and slid into his hair having clearly found a weak point in the bubble which mostly repelled them.

"Get them off. Call them off, can't you," he yelled at Vervain, whilst swirling on the spot in order to face his molester. Raven sucked in a deep breath. She was a child of no more than thirteen, and for a moment he glimpsed her as she had been, plump and rosy with long coils of golden hair. The illusion lasted but a second. It burst revealing her for the cadaver she now was.

"Scared, demon," Jaku spat from a few yards away. There was no love lost between them despite Raven's decision to free the demon-hunter. The gash in his thigh from where Jaku had implanted the shard of broken china still itched like hell if he let his thoughts stray for more than a second. However, Jaku's release had made sense in context. Only Skaa had challenged the decision. Raven had simply ignored his protest. The truth was, Jaku was the best person for the job. He'd made an impassioned plea to be included in the mission to seek out Asha's Ti-spirit and return it to her in the hopes of reviving her from death. He also knew both Asha and Vervain better than any of the Prince's elite guard who might have been persuaded to come along.

Rather than rise to the implication of cowardice, Raven fixed Jaku with a cold stare. The man looked absolutely ghastly, far worse than some of the corpses leering out of the gloom. He'd plastered on more make-up than a business magnate's chief squeeze, but he hadn't tried to cover his recent burns. Instead, he'd left them, patches of vivid red skin; cracks in his otherwise perfect veneer.

A broken doll.

Damaged.

He suspected that's how Jaku saw himself now, too. Why else volunteer for a suicide mission to help your enemy? Assuming they were actually undertaking the mission and this wasn't some human ploy to take him out and peddle his ass to the nearest backstreet alchemist.

He turned away from Jaku, who would have made a good gargoyle considering how still he managed to keep and returned his focus to Vervain, only for his stomach to lurch.

"Aw, that's just nasty."

The copse-man appeared to be kissing one of the bloody ghouls, and the damn thing had lit up like a firefly from the contact.

"Hold your tongue," Vervain called when the glowing spirit eventually danced free of his hold. "There are protocols to follow, demon. If you can't respect them, I can't guarantee your safety. We need permission to enter the Death Ward after dark."

The honourable dead never rescinded on a bargain. At least, those were the rumours.

"Then please, call the gate guard instead of wooing and let's get on with this."

Vervain cast back his cowl so that the rosy glow of the moonlight shone upon his shaven pate. He turned his head and smiled. No longer the black orbs they were in daylight, his piercing eyes were now lit from within. The black transformed into white, ringed with lime-green flames.

"It's already done."

On cue, a figure seeped into the space between the gates. Amorphous and different to the other spectres; it seemed to bend the moonlight around it, so that it appeared clothed in a cloak of shimmering silver. The scent of pine needles smouldering under the sun filled Raven's nostrils.

"Who seeks entry at the Gates of the Dead?"

"I do." Vervain stepped forward. "I seek permission to walk-between."

What passed for the ghoul's elongated head hunched towards them, stretching as it seemed to sniff the air, before snapping back to its former pose. "You bring petitioners in addition to your person tonight, Vervain. Do they also seek to walk-between?"

"Aye, that is so."

"To what end? One of those with you is known to my princes, and they express concern for the fates of their eternal subjects. What assurance do you provide that he'll behave? And the other, what possible purpose have the youkai among us?"

Jaku was not welcome here. Hm, that was a titbit of information he could have done with knowing before they got here. Now however, didn't seem the time to bring it up.

"We intend no harm to your subjects, only to address a single, unfettered soul. The demon is with us because the spirit was beloved of his master and he wishes to impart those regards. As for assurances, I can offer only my word, and pray it is still good."

"We will take a drop of your blood. Do you accept?"

"I do."

The bubble around them immediately burst allowing the gathered spirits to press close, dividing them. Conquer would be a matter of moments. Raven locked his arms fast against his sides and did his utmost to ignore the throttling choke-hold around his neck and the claws raking across his thighs.

The spectral gate guard stretched once more, becoming impossibly tall and conical. Its head seemed to shrink while the hem of its robe billowed wide.

Crystals started splintering inside Raven's head, not from the lack of oxygen, but from the new, ear-drum-perforating sound of the spectre's cackle. That alone forced him to raise his arms into order to clasp them over his ears.

He never wanted to hear another spirit laugh.

Ever.

"So, the old tales are true?" Each syllable of the eerie cackle resembled an icicle being thrust into his ear. "Why not, my princes say. Why not— indeed? Yes, come in through our doors. You are welcome. Most welcome. We await the unfolding of deeds."

"We're in," Jaku hissed beneath his breath. "Yes!" His fist clenched in triumph.

Raven didn't share his joy. All they'd done was mount the first hurdle, and he didn't care for the welcome speech.

However, the gates were now thrown wide.

The wind puffed up again and sucked them into its chilly embrace. Scooped up and thrust down. Raven landed hard on his arse in a frozen wasteland. Only the grey of Raven's robe and the black of Jaku's elaborate outfit broke up the white monotony.

White, as far as the eye could see.

Cold in the air. A billowing fog obscured all but a few inches of the horizon.

The ground crackled as he moved.

Winter frost lay underfoot.

Jaku's long coat flapped behind him like wings as he trod a circle around Raven and Vervain. "We're roughly central. Get up. We'll try right first."

Vervain stooped and offered Raven a hand up from the floor.

"How does he know where we are? Raven asked, having gained his feet. Jaku, already several steps ahead, was rapidly disappearing.

Vervain sucked his thumb into his mouth, removing a smear of blood from across the tip. A single drop lay like a ruby buried in the snow. "The land here doesn't change. Jaku spent his childhood wandering the graveyard at night. Right will take us to the crypt that belongs to Asha's family I believe. It's the obvious place to start. The ties of kinship are important to the dead, more so than they are to the living. We may find her lingering there awaiting the entombment of her body."

Frankly, he couldn't picture Asha loitering anywhere without an express purpose, and if the Ti-spirit was the personality, there didn't seem any reason why death would have changed things. Then again, the aftermath of human death was a subject on which his knowledge was decidedly sketchy. Youkai deaths were altogether simpler affairs.

"Wait up, Jaku." Vervain swung a leather satchel out from beneath his robe, and from it took several metres of tubing which he slotted together to form a long pole. The last three pieces formed a triangle, which supported a large net. "Here, make yourself useful, carry this." He thrust the net upon Raven.

Scowling seemed the only logical answer. He'd rather have his hands free than carry a net, and besides, "Surely spirit hunting requires something more substantial than a butterfly net."

Vervain gave an enigmatic shrug. "Trust me, demon, I know my job. I've seen countless deaths and countless more spirits. Certain things are almost inevitable, and it pays to be prepared. I'll be as pleased as you if we find her sitting preening on a bench and happy to indulge in a quiet chat, but death borne of violence doesn't generally make for a happy ghost."

Okay, but that still didn't explain the net.

Vervain turned away, obviously believing their conversation done. Apprehensively, Raven followed. He couldn't tell if they were trekking north, south or in a figure of eight. The entire landscape appeared to consist of acres of frozen lawn. When they stumbled upon a row of perfectly frozen violets, he crushed several in the hope of leaving a trail, but within moments the ice had reformed and the landmark dissolved back into the fog.

"Wouldn't it have been easier for us to have

flown in, given that you know the position of her family crypt?"

Jaku mumbled something under his breath, which Raven prompted him to repeat.

"I said you'd never have made it to ground level. Recall our entrance."

Okay, so it had been a stupid suggestion, but he was definitely leaving by that route. Protocol be damned. He had no intention of wandering about for hours trying to find the gate.

Jaku's lecture continued, "The only reason we're still breathing is because of Vervain. They tolerate and respect him, even if they don't exactly like him."

He stopped abruptly and turned left, sending his finery swirling about his person and sweeping up the powdery slivers of frost. His head turned this way and that, finally settling upon a single direction.

"This way, I think. Past the moon dial and the enclosure should be on the left. There's a wooden door set into a high hedge."

They reached said hedge in another few paces and followed the overgrown monster until they reached the gate, an oak, iron-hinged structure straight out of a dungeon. Snowberries and a dogwood threaded through tangle of privet branches, while wild frozen brambles hung like huge gemstones. There were no small mammals or birds here to eat them.

"Locked?" Vervain asked, pushing up his sleeves.

Jaku grasped the iron hasp and gave it a sharp turn. He shook his head as the gate swung inwards, the aged, rusted hinges screeching in alarm.

"She's here."

Raven sensed it too—a wash of fear that rolled like ice-water down his back, but which had nothing to do with anxiety or anticipation, just the sense of her presence.

The spirit, Asha, lingered some distance off, on the very edge of his perceptions, but its anger and anguish bled into the ether around it. Her Ti soul was strong, as was necessary for a queen. For the first time he genuinely believed they could make this happen. He could restore his prince's lover and hence gain a queen. Before this, he'd craved that eventuality but never truly expected it to happen. They were dabbling in what the humans called black arts. The prospect for gain was good, but at what price?

Sensing a reluctance to engage from the two men, Raven hoisted the net aloft and pushed past Jaku. If a net was what it took, then best he lead. No sense in waiting for their presence to be discovered. If you were going to attack something in its lair, best do it while it slept.

Strategy... They needed a strategy. They'd come here with so little forward planning.

The notion of a making this a simple search and rescue fled along with his first glimpse of what she'd become. Raven stopped dead in his tracks.

Asha—porcelain perfect in life. She might have been his hereditary enemy but he could still appreciate her visual appeal. Even in the heat of battle she'd been impossibly lovely. Now, all evidence of grace had gone. Lost, along with her body.

"No, that's not possible. How can it? It can't..." He stared at her, then at Vervain, and finally at the net.

"She's as I feared." Vervain briefly covered his eyes.

Her. It. Raven gawped at the winged head, unable to equate it with the raw emotional image of his prince still curled around the body of his dead queen. This monstrosity couldn't be her, but when it turned, saw them, looked him straight in the eye, then he couldn't hide from the truth.

"Asha?" Her name escaped his lips as a soft murmur, but the whisper carried on the breeze gaining volume.

She rushed straight towards him.

Raven ducked.

"Catch her," Vervain bellowed. "Keep your focus."

Catch it. He wanted to hide from it, this monstrosity carved of nightmares. He'd seen horrors and wonders enough to draw the sanity from most human brains. Yet this outweighed them all. He kept staring at it, mesmerised by its grotesque beauty and aching familiarity. Humans were not meant for such transformations. He and Asha had never been friends, but they'd reached an understanding. A joint love of Blaze had given them common ground. All that was gone now. He saw only the cruel expression hewn from once perfect features, and the mouth opening impossibly wide. Three rows of needle-like teeth, over which flicked a tongue as black as soot. He couldn't present Blaze with this. He had to go back and tell him it was over, the link broken, Asha gone.

She zipped over their heads, banked left and made a second pass before taking flight towards the far end of the secluded compound. Jaku and Vervain immediately shot off after it. "Come on," they barked.

Raven hung back. "I can't... Blaze can't see that."

"Blaze doesn't need to. That's why we didn't bring him. She suffered a major trauma, you idiot. You didn't actually imagine she'd be pottering about looking all wan and fey, did you? Did you?" Jaku's voice grew louder with each word. "Get moving with that net."

Two wary paces forward and Raven watched the spirit emerge from behind a statue of a mother and child. It swooped down heading for the back of Vervain's neck. Jaku came tearing after it.

"Look out," Raven yelled as he launched himself forward with the net. Stretched to his limits, the muscles in his thighs groaning at the exertion, he swept the net over arm and down, missed completely, and entangled Vervain instead. The spirit took a bite out of the Death Warden's scalp.

"Bitch!" Vervain hollered.

"Watch how you're talking to my queen," Raven bellowed in response, suddenly feeling light-hearted in this pit of hell. He freed Vervain from the net and they both took off after it again. The damned thing was zippy as a whippet. When they caught up with Jaku, they found him playing a complicated game of wind the bobbin with it and his halberd.

"Get out of the way." Vervain shoved them both into the hedge. His white-green eyes were aglow. Blood flowed in a thick stream down the side of his face, and had soaked into the cowl of his robe. He cracked his knuckles, and then words in the ancient tongue spilled from his lips.

"No," Raven thundered, as he extracted himself from the bush. There was a reason why the use of that particular language had fallen out of favour. It caused rents in the fabric of the world. It made things real that should never have been and undid things that should already have happened. No denying it was powerful, but it was also dangerous, and ought not to be messed with by tinkering amateurs. "What are you doing, you fool?"

"He speaks the old tongue," Jaku's guard lapsed a moment while he plucked a privet needle from one of his elaborate braids.

Raven shoved him back into the thicket of snowberries, which popped as he landed upon them. "He might speak it but his diction is crap, and it's not something you want to risk getting wrong."

Too late, the magic left Vervain's hands, misfired, and reduced the mother and baby statue into powdered ruins.

God job they hadn't made any promises about leaving the décor intact.

"Bollocks!" Vervain cursed.

"How about we focus on coaxing her, instead of obliteration?" Raven scolded.

"Fine. Then give me the net." Pissed off and

covered in snowberry pulp, Jaku snatched the net from Raven's hands. About to retaliate, Raven stopped short as his vision blurred. Not again. He didn't need a reminder. He already knew how this ended.

"Give me back the net, Jaku." He tempered his voice, spoke as softly as his husky tones would allow. "She knows you. She's more likely to listen. You need to do the coaxing. Give me the net and you reel her in."

Jaku hesitated, clearly torn. Finally, he handed back the net.

Raven and Vervain withdrew behind a statue of a swan the size of a pony. "Sit this one out, copse-man." He tore a large leaf off one of the bushes and passed it over. "Concentrate on stemming the bleeding. I don't know much, but I know the dead like blood and so do I, and right now, you reek of it."

Leaf clasped tightly to his head, Vervain slumped onto the grass. "Be careful of her. She's both stronger and more fragile than she looks."

"Just reassure me before I do this that we're going to get the whole personality back, not just the nasty bits once we reunite all the parts."

"More or less. It's a delicate process."

That would have to do. At least it wasn't an outright no, or worse, an outrageous lie.

Raven skirted the inside edge of the compound. Not quite so thick here, the mist peeled back in places allowing him glimpses of stone urns and in one corner the marble mausoleum that housed generations of Lemarches. He kept to the shadows, following the swish and crackle of Jaku's footsteps over the permafrost.

Jaku kept talking; the low murmur of his words constantly rolling on the breeze. Slowly, surely he was reeling her in. Raven need only be ready to—

Dive.

The net swept wide, missing her again, this time by mere inches. The unwieldy weapon didn't make for a speedy recovery, even with his strength. By the time he'd reversed his swing and turned around the bitch was right behind him.

A snake of prehensile hair entwined around his extended arm and started to weave its way up, finding a way through the plates of his leather armour to reach around his neck. Raven dropped the net, but rather than using his free hands to rip at the strands constricting his throat, he instead used hand over hand on her hair to drag her closer. "The net," he barked at Jaku, thinking a sack might be better.

"Got her!" Jaku screamed. Teeth gritted he gingerly lowered the net to the ground. Raven knelt alongside. From out of a sheath he pulled a knife and began cutting his way through the strands of inky black hair. The bodiless beastie remained frighteningly still inside the net.

"We haven't killed it, have we?" He wasn't sure if the dead could die again?

"She's sleeping." Vervain crawled towards them from out of the mist. "It's a spirit net. It's designed for the job. She shouldn't give us any trouble now, until we get back to the castle."

"What I don't understand is how she can feel so solid." Raven ran the soft strands of hair he'd cut across his palm. They still bore the trace of her scent. "I thought the whole point was these Ti-spirits are bodiless and they hunger for what they've lost."

"It's your mind that makes her solid." Vervain shuffled forward and crushed the netting flat beneath his knees. "Her appearances is really only a psychic impression. How strong she is depends entirely on how much credit you give her. It was a hard fight, because none of us expected any less of her. I think it's fair to say she'd have given us a similar run around in life."

"She'd not thank you for crushing her like that." Jaku pushed Vervain off the net, but instead of staying flat, the sides bulged around the shape of the head again. Presumably there was a name for the type of spirit Asha had become. Vervain had come prepared. He had to have encountered such beings before, but now didn't seem the time to ask. Instead Raven watched Jaku snap a ribbon off his exotic coat and tie it around the open end of the net. Having then set it carefully aside, he dismantled the pole and handed it back to Vervain.

"Let's see to your head," Raven offered, shuffling over to Vervain. The wound, despite signs of clotting around the edges wouldn't quit leaking. His heart rate surged at the sniff of blood. His mouth opened around a low groan. Vervain backed away from him warily.

"Hey, it's okay. I have my appetites under control." Still, all the programming in the world couldn't completely override base instincts. His nostrils flared as Jaku set a large piece of gauze dressing over Vervain's wound. Raven turned his back. While the other two men got to their feet, Raven stole a surreptitious lick of blood off the discarded leaf. The copse-man tasted good, a little more piquant than the average human, although that might have been down to the adrenaline and all the endorphins floating through his veins at the moment. Pain did tend to sharpen the taste.

"All set?"

Raven nodded. He remained at the rear as they retraced their steps to the iron-hinged gate. Any more trouble and he was grabbing the head and making a quick getaway. He'd faced quite enough ghouls for one night. Besides, he couldn't trust the idiots up at the castle not to attempt something radical or stupid, or even radical and stupid in his absence. He didn't want to get back to find a castle full of Floraces.

"Well met, Vervain." The lyrical voice drifted to them out of the mist beyond the gate. Clearly they should have already flown.

For several moments, Raven squinted, attempting to pick out shapes but seeing nothing, then abruptly the petals of fog peeled away, revealing a cluster of knights on horseback. Humans hadn't dressed like that since the days of his youth, centuries ago.

"Oh shit!" The curse escaped from between Jaku's gritted teeth. He clutched the net bag tightly to his chest, which unfortunately only served to draw attention to it.

Vervain gave a low and elaborate bow. "Your highnesses. You do us great honour."

"While you take us for fools," said the foremost of the princes. "We granted safe passage to walk-between, not a licence to assault and kidnap our treasured and loyal subjects. Do you think we don't see what occurs in our realm?"

A deep grimace suffused Vervain's face. He paled significantly.

A younger prince stepped forward, this one dressed in red and gold, with an enormous peacock feathered hat. "Don't fret, copse-man, it isn't you we seek. Your work mostly pleases us. Our ire is at another."

"Me?" Jaku's voice cracked as he spoke, so the single word barely sounded.

They turned as one towards him, and the young prince beckoned him forward.

"No." Vervain caught hold of Jaku's sleeve and held him back. "Did we not settle this long ago? Is it not done? You took his family."

"We took nothing. The sacrifice was their choice. We demanded nothing of them."

"Leave it, Vervain." Jaku gently lowered the net bag. He placed his hand on top of Vervain's and gently uncurled the copse-man's fingers from the fabric. "This is how it should be. It's how it always should have been. They were my mistakes. I didn't want anyone else to pay for them then, and nor do I wish that now. I know I said otherwise at the time, but I knew what I was doing. And to whom I was doing it."

"Careful of your words," Vervain cautioned in anguish.

Raven scooped up the bag.

"I'm only stating what they already know to be true." Jaku turned to the thirteen princes again, this time stepping forward until he stood only a few feet from the horses' forelocks. "Let Vervain and this demon take Asha. She has the chance to gain what you crave. Prove you are neither jealous nor cruel. I will stay in her place."

Lights ignited inside twenty-six hungry eyes. Raven had seen demons starved of blood in the heat of frenzy, but even that couldn't compare with the yearning etched into the faces of the dead.

"We will feed on you. Devour you whole."

Jaku inclined his head. Perhaps the glint of tears soiled his eyelashes. He stood proud, shoulders back. A wry smile creased his fire-scarred face. "My Ci'th will not sustain you. I will be gone, but you will be no more alive."

"I still question what a demon wants with a penanggalan?" said a bearded prince, dressed in pale blue.

"Who cares," replied the first. "I hunger for his vein."

"As do I." The echo of similar sentiments filled the air.

"Jaku, please reconsider. Asha would not have wanted you to sacrifice yourself in this way."

Raven grasped Vervain's wrist before he could tug Jaku back from the ravenous throng. "This is his desire, copse-man. It's the truth of him. Don't deny him his sacrifice." He lowered his voice a fraction and leaned in closer to Vervain. The smell of blood and fear still rolled off the copse-man in waves. "He no longer desires this life. Everything he cares about is gone. Even if Asha is restored, she is lost to him. He'll never befriend Blaze."

"But they will tear him apart. I can't stand idly by and watch that."

"It will be quick." He smiled grimly. "Dare I say even merciful?"

"Accept the deal, Vervain." Jaku turned beseechingly. Like the princes, hunger marked his face. He craved relief. "Take Asha to her lover. I'm glad she found someone worthy with whom to share her soul, even though I cannot agree with the choice. I return to my family now. Should these ghouls allow it then stow my bones in the old way; an ossuary, I will stand guard."

Dejection bowed Vervain's shaven head. "I'll do what I can." He cast his arms around Jaku's shoulders in a solemn embrace. "Be at peace." They both kept their farewells brief. What use was there in prolonging the moment? The night was lengthening, and there remained much still to accomplish.

"Goodbye, demon," Jaku remarked. They exchanged no hugs or handshakes. "I'm glad I shan't live to see you rule. The Earth was never meant to be your home."

Raven gave him a curt nod, and then he swept Vervain up into his arms and kicked high into the air. The breeze caught his wings as he shifted shape, and he beat them hard, until they soared high above the mist. The blood moon was at its zenith. It was past time that they marched to war.

6. MOON RISE

**

"Act respectfully and provide wisely for the deceased,
unless you plan to welcome them into your home."
–Mrs Tunney's Manual of Good Household Practice.

**

NEAR EXHAUSTED BY the flight, Raven dropped Vervain onto the balcony of the Hall of Shadows, and then slumped alongside. Next time he was definitely sticking to the bridge. The flight while carrying Vervain in his arms had just about torn his flight muscles to pieces.

He released the sack containing Asha's head, so that it sat between them and heaved in a deep breath. Slowly he stretched his tired wings and let them slide back into his skin.

"Now what do we do?" he asked. The smell of smouldering rose petals permeated the air coming from the ill-lit room beyond the latticework screening. "How do we make her whole again, Vervain?" They'd not discussed matters much beyond the retrieval of her Ti-soul.

The copse-man pushed himself into a seated position and shrugged the frost from his shoulders. The winter climate of the Death Ward had persisted all the way to the castle.

"There are no guarantees in this. We're following a script, and not a script I'm familiar with. I'm neither an alchemist nor a demonologist."

"I can provide both of those things." Indeed they were already on hand. From the corner of his eye, Raven watched Skaa emerge from the shadows. Then Sorrow parted form from his brother's silhouette. The pair had clearly been on the battlements keeping a look out for their return. "What else do we need?"

Interesting. The copse-man's robe seemed decidedly plain and grey up here. There were no fanciful faces peeping from within the weft as there had been in the City. Then again, there wasn't a plethora of human ghosts up here.

"Chemicals. Space to work. Ink. You've already restored the physical head to her body, so that is good. We'll also need Blaze to be present."

That was just as well since the chances of parting him from Asha's side for more than a millisecond were virtually zero. Come to think of it, he wasn't going to let them get anywhere near her.

"We don't actually need Blaze conscious, do we?" He grimaced uneasily.

Sorrow and Skaa's expressions echoed his unease. None of them wanted to risk being turned into another demon bowling ball. He almost enquired as to Florian and Grace's wellbeing, but changed his mind. It would only cause an unnecessary distraction.

Addressing one problem at a time, that was the way forward.

"Consent is always preferable," Vervain replied in a dry drawl. He pushed himself onto his feet and looked around them, all shadows and teeth and hunger. "However, he's your prince not mine. Your choice. His presence is what's important not his state of consciousness."

"How did you knock him out on the way back from the warehouse?"

Sorrow slouched against the balustrade. He'd changed outfits again, opting for a bottle green three piece suit with tails. He'd showered off all the soot too, and his dark hair shone like strips of black satin in the torchlight. "I don't think you're going to get close enough to smack him over the head. Just saying..."

Raven worried a loose piece of skin on his lips. True, he'd accidentally on purpose knocked Blaze's head against a warehouse wall or two on their flight back to the castle but things had been pretty desperate. Smoke from the fires Blaze had started still blotted out most of the cityscape below. Where there were gaps, there were flames. Only the Death Ward and the Heights remained entirely unaffected.

"Ether," Skaa's sibilant whisper perfectly mimicked the hiss of gas leaking from a pipe. He slithered fully into view, casting off his cloak of shadows. "We can funnel it in, just enough to make him woozy, and then you can knock him out. I've been using it to herd the grubs around. It makes them a little nauseous, nothing worse. He should stomach it fine."

THE ONLY SURPRISING thing about the plan was that it worked straight off without mishap. Hoisting a limb each, Raven and Vervain lifted Blaze onto a makeshift workbench after he collapsed from inhaling a nice dose of ether. They positioned Asha's body alongside him. Vervain maintained it would be better if they were kept together so as to cement the bond.

The strange chemical odour still lingered in the air around them. Raven gasped a little as he released his hold on Blaze. Then he went to swallow some water. When he returned, Sorrow and Skaa were wheeling racks of alchemical components into the room on huge trolleys. As far as he could tell with his limited alchemical knowledge most of the gubbins consisted of chemical solutions, but a bobbin full of steel thread also featured along with a large array of surgical instruments. Why the brothers considered those necessary he couldn't imagine. They certainly weren't going near Blaze with them.

"We weren't certain over exactly what you wanted so we brought what we thought we might need."

"That's fine. They'll be wonderful." Vervain breezed around the table, prodding at the occasional bit of exposed flesh.

Raven picked up one of the bottles and read the label: "Embalming Fluid", and another: "Nascent Carbuncle Irregularities". Neither sounded terribly appropriate.

"Strip off his clothes. I need his upper body uncovered. You'll have to expose her neck, too. The stitching won't be enough. We're going to have to bind her head in place with runes. Can't have it coming loose on state parades and causing a ghastly fuss." Vervain gave a little chuckle. His eyes were positively alight. His focus riveted upon the task.

Raven slapped him across the back before he set to work following instructions. He'd decided he liked the Death Warden. There was something about his macabre sense of humour that tickled him. He could well imagine Vervain sharing a drink and a snack over Blaze's comatose body. He figured the guy was used to stationary humans and pickling their remains, or whatever it was they did with them. Something to do with mahogany boxes he believed.

Raven stroked a hand through the fine strands of Blaze's golden hair, smoothing them back into place after he'd removed his clothing. His prince was sleeping like a babe, which ironed out some of the signs of grief from his face. He traced two fingers over Blaze's lips before stepping back to allow Vervain space to work.

The copse-man snatched up a box of fish hooks from the trolley and started feeding them through Blaze's skin over strategic points. Raven winced on Blaze's behalf. Just because they had rapid healing didn't make the discomfort any less. The hooks were soon fastened to wires that laced across his torso which were strung with a multitude of charms.

"Just a few precautions," Vervain reassured him. The copse-man had long agile fingers that made quick work of the procedure. "We're doing this because he's precious, right?"

"And because he's a fool," Skaa added. "I still don't know why we're considering bowing to a human queen."

"She's hardly that any more, Skaa." Raven retorted.

The assassin simply buried his nose in the text Vervain had produced, which detailed a theoretic procedure for the process of restoring the Ti to the body in order to revisit the moments of death. They were hoping since Asha's Ci'th soul was still present in Blaze that once restored her Ti spirit would stay put. The chemical mixture it required, eventually solidified into a straw-coloured gloop he had to smear over every visible bit of Blaze and Asha's skin.

If Blaze woke unexpectedly, he was going to hog roast them all for this. He'd protested the bronzer. This was infinitely worse. It bore the consistency of snot and smelled of tulips and turpentine. The latter, he suspected to be the base.

"Okay, I think we're done. Now it's just a matter of forcing her Ti spirit back into her body."

Vervain stepped back from the table and folded his arms, so that his hands disappeared inside his sleeves.

"Which we do how?" Raven lifted his shoulder in a questioning shrug. Unlike the other three he hadn't been given the opportunity to pour over the text. "I mean what if she doesn't want to? What if she likes being a flying head?"

Skaa's velvet-black eyes widened. "You brought a penanggalan here? That's what's in the sack. Those bitches are like... I thought we were talking about releasing her from a soul jar or something."

Vervain slapped a rune wafer to his forehead, which momentarily shut Skaa up. He did the same for Sorrow, Raven, and himself. Blaze he marked in a different way, covering his torso and face in black ink, while Asha he marked with bold runes all around her neck.

"A soul jar is something you have to construct for yourself. Demons!" Vervain shook his head. "You'd think considering how long you all live you might find time for a book or two."

"Watch your words, copse-man," Skaa leered at him evilly.

Raven positioned himself between them. "What next?"

"We withdraw and release her. We'll just need a drop or two of..." He paused and dug into the depths of his robe. From out of a pocket he produced a small ornate vial. A smile lit his craggy face. "Yes, this. This will do fine. It's good to think ahead. It should definitely pique her interest."

He smeared the contents over Asha's lips and tongue and left a tantalising trail of drips between the bodies and the sack. "Everybody out. Raven, release her."

Release her. Holy shit! He shook Asha's Ti-spirit out of the bag and ran; figuring the bitch likely had it in for him.

L IKE FOUR SACRED children, they huddled together behind the screen, their foreheads pressed to the fretwork, eyes burning through lack of blinking.

"Why isn't it following the trail?" Raven asked. Ten minutes had passed and Asha's Ti hadn't shown the faintest bit of interest in either of the bodies on the table.

"How am I supposed to know?" Vervain turned away and pressed his back to the screen. "We did everything. It's like she can't sense him. Something must be off."

"Those chemicals were fresh," both brothers insisted. The remark prompted another souring of Vervain's craggy features. He scratched at his bald pate, then dug in his pocket for the empty vial and sniffed at the residue in the bottom. His brow furrowed as though someone had sunk a stone into his brain.

"What is that anyway?" Raven asked.

Vervain worked his little finger around the neck of the bottle. "Evidently not what I hoped to find in there. I suspected, but I hoped given it was the final ingredient we needed."

'What is it?"

"Demon seed."

"You mean his... When did you get that?" Casting his mind back over events, Raven couldn't recall a time when Blaze and Vervain had been alone. So the exchange must have happened before they'd found him. He made a mental note to advise Blaze against parting with such gifts in the future. Then again, maybe his liege had already realised that.

"I didn't. Whatever this is, it isn't Blaze's seed.

That's the point. It's why she's whizzing around in there like a top and not reconnecting like she's supposed to. This isn't his."

"Give me that." Raven upended the dregs of the vial into his mouth. "Nah, definitely not Blaze." He sucked on his tongue a bit. His nose wrinkled. "It's not even..." He stuck out his tongue, and then dragged it back in again. "It sort of smells like Blaze, but it tastes more like wax."

It only took a single glance at Blaze and his lovely sculpted blond spikes to make the connection.

"He gave me hair wax," Vervain boomed in outrage. "The sly... Oh, never mind. I'll deal with that problem later. The cheeky bastard. Right now, we need one of his essences in order to attract her attention. Semen would be best, but tears or blood would serve."

"Well, if you think any of us are going in there to give him a knuckle shuffle you're mistaken," Sorrow remarked.

Despite the sly looks from the others in his direction, Raven absolutely concurred on that point. Under no circumstances was he going anywhere near Asha's Ti-spirit. He'd had one encounter too many with it already.

"We'll have to cut him."

Damn, he couldn't believe he was making this suggestion either.

"Blood will definitely work, won't it? You said any of the essential essences, right?"

Vervain nodded. "Blood will serve; it just might not be so pleasant for him in the long run. I mean it's probably not the exact taste of him he'd prefer for her to have."

"Youkai," muttered Sorrow. "Blood sharing doesn't concern us."

Vervain eyed him distastefully. "Freshly drawn blood then," he agreed.

Skaa drew a long narrow pipe from a channel sewn into his leather armour and fit a dart into one end. He slotted the pipe carefully through a hole in the latticework screen. "Ah, Blaze. You don't know how often I've longed to do this."

The point of the dart struck Blaze's hand. He twitched in his slumber, causing the feathered dart to fall out. Asha's consciousness swooped towards it immediately. A blood droplet leaked from the puncture wound and splashed against her cheek. Her eyes closed and she inhaled sharply, whereupon all the tension and cruelty momentarily vanished from her expression. She seemed content. Then an impossibly long tongue swept out to lick up the blood.

"Yes," Vervain hissed in triumph. "She's recognised him."

She sucked at the tiny puncture wound until the blood stopped flowing. Her eyes narrowed thoughtfully at that point and her wings carried her up onto the table. She hovered over Blaze's chest.

Behind the screen they all held their breath as she sniffed at both the bodies. Blaze certainly held the greater fascination, but then it seemed she drew too close to her own physical form. Her spirit form lost its shape, became stretched and thinned. It grew distorted as though it were being pulled in the direction of her body and sucked in through the nostrils. The wings on her head flapped, but no amount of frantic motion could pull her free of the sucking tide. Thinner and thinner it drew her, elongating her narrow face from chin to crown until only a slender thread remained. Raven peeked through his right eye. The penanggalan had gone. The only remnant of her was a sooty stain around the nose of Asha's corpse.

"Is it done? Is she fixed? What happened? Did we fuck up?"

Asha's eyes snapped open.

"It worked." Vervain shook hands with Skaa and Sorrow, but Raven's muscles remained tensed.

"Did it?" he asked. He watched as Asha lurched upright and straddled Blaze's prone form. They might have animated her corpse, but he wasn't entirely sure Asha was truly herself once more.

7. OUT COLD

BLAZE STIRRED IN his bed as someone walked their fingers up his thigh. Irritably, he batted at the annoyance, only for the caress to climb to his stomach and trace the intricate loops and flourishes of the large tattoo that covered most of his abdomen. Higher still, the touch lingered over one nipple, before settling over his heart, where the raised and mottled form of an ancient sigil was burned into the flesh.

"Asha," he sighed. "Asha, is that you, my love?" His eyes fluttered open in time to see her join the sigil burned into her own palm tightly to the one on his chest. Energy pulsed between them. It rushed upwards out of his chest, leaving his body cold, while a faint purple-edged glow twisted around her arm, until its tendrils licked her slender throat.

"Blaze," she purred, and just the sound of her voice sent a ripple of pleasure through his loins—

soft pleasure, so different to the bite of her nails upon his chest.

"How are you here? How can you be here?" he asked, convinced this was a pleasant dream.

"You tell me, Demon Prince. You're in control of this mess." Her eyes flared green and strangely luminescent in the half-light.

He wasn't in control. He barely knew which day it was, or what season.

Dark memories stirred, and tore through the veil of slumber that still clouded his mind.

This—her being here, wasn't possible. Talon had seen to that when he'd taken her from him. Yet it was her face staring down at him, entrancing him with the same flawless perfection that had captured his interest the very first time they'd met. She ought to be still lying cold beside him. He stared at her cherry-red lips, recalling the taste of her, the smell of her dark hair, and the way those ebony locks felt draped across his skin when they made love. Currently, she wore her hair bound in an elaborate knot, decorated with glinting white-gems.

"Asha." He strained upwards to reach and kiss her, but her palm remained fast against his chest, the glowing sigils still binding them.

"Sex and flesh, isn't that the demon way?" Her nails continued to bite into his skin, leaving behind ruddy half-moon impressions. "Isn't this what you wanted from the start? To have complete control," she lowered her head and licked a line up the side of his throat, stopping shy of his ear, "or at least the illusion of it." She nuzzled closer, tormenting him with delicate kisses, though no breath tickled his skin. She nipped his earlobe hard, drawing blood, which tickled as it rolled down his neck and onto her tongue. "Surely you didn't expect to steal my soul and give nothing in return?"

"I expected nothing. Asha—if I'd known. You have to believe me." He reached up and cupped the gentle curve of her cheek. Beneath the lace edge of her dress, he spied black sigils ringing the base of her throat.

The tinkling uneasy sound of Asha's laughter rippled across his senses, and shattered the glass by his bedside. He turned his head to avoid the splinters, but one struck his temple, leaving a bloody nick that she swooped down to lick.

She grabbed one wrist and pinned it by the side of his head, the other hand remained splayed across the brand upon his chest. "I've borne unimaginable pain for you. It's your turn to know that agony now." She tore her hand from his chest, ripping the two sigils apart and cutting the flow of energy between them, leaving him light-headed as she slid her palm down over the firm contours of his abdomen to the sensitive spot between his navel and his groin. "Submit to me, Blaze. Just submit."

As if there were anything else he could give. He was hers already. He had been since the moment they'd met. Her cool poised indifference had entranced him more thoroughly than any obvious erotic display. He'd let her allure cloud his reasoning, until he'd become enslaved by his need to be with her, had allowed the fire that raged between them to drive events when control would have served them better. Still, he couldn't undo the past, or her memory, nor was he sure he wanted to. He didn't want to lose that passion, the level of closeness.

Even now, the scent of her, so close, and her presence above him coaxed his already taxed senses. The borders between reality and desire wavered. Blaze growled at the slow undulation of her body against his. The demon within demanded satisfaction, so that sweat beaded across his body.

Mine, his heart screamed. My love. My soul mate. My queen.

His for eternity.

The heat rising from his skin steeped them both in sweat, and brought the faintest hint of colour to her chalk-white cheeks.

"I love you, Blaze," she whispered into his mouth, just before their lips met. "But now you have to burn. Set the world alight." Her palm closed around the length of his shaft where it lay sandwiched between their bodies. "Burn..." Her thumb traced a slow circle around the flared head of his cock, making his pulse race. Each touch was pure agony. He already burned, with his need for her and the desperation he felt to bury himself inside her. She didn't need to set him alight. That was already done.

"Burn..."

He didn't need the flames, and the wild fire. He already felt too much of both.

"Stop. Please, Asha. I don't want to hurt you. I've hurt you enough already."

Her hand continued to work, rubbing, drawing pleasure from him, so that even though it hurt he couldn't help but grind his hips against her.

Every nerve in his body leapt as she swept her thumb over the delicate slit. He stopped thinking in terms of black and white. His sight skewed. Then a blood red vision swam across the inside of his eyelids. Explosive orange splashed across blank white walls of his mind, and her smile became a flash of purple that melted slowly into lilac.

"Burn, Blaze. Burn." Her teeth slid into the soft flesh of his neck. Perfect pain surged through every neural pathway. The sound of two heartbeats pounded like duelling drums in his ears. Fever enveloped him, but even as he welcomed the bittersweet cloud of release, his body tensed at the fear of the encroaching darkness.

"Burn..." Her whisper faded from his ears.

The sky was no longer black...

It was yellow and grey. Ash swirled in the air like snowflakes, as pretty as the blood speckled snow that covered the roof tiles. He stood on the cathedral roof, the whole of the city spread around him. Blaze stared at his bloodied hands in dismay. Everything he thought he had was gone. He couldn't rewind time and make things sane again. Forked lightning pierced the sky. A blue streamer poured along the apex of the roof and into him. It surged up his spine, filling him with an uncontrollable amount of energy.

Across the city, the Birdcage was alight. The entirety of the Eyrie lit up like a warning beacon. Screams and the clash of arms filled the streets below.

"Asha," he called, bewildered by all that flowed

around him. He stretched out his hands, but nobody took them. Nobody offered him comfort.

He was utterly alone.

"Asha!"

His dejection found no end. Blaze closed his eyes. The licking flames inside his eyelids continued to dance. He snapped his eyes open again, coming to attention, as a single word passed his lips, "Burn."

8: SHADOW QUEEN

**

"Thus do their souls join
and form the Triumvirate."
Entropy for Fun and Profit.
**

BURN...

Hell and eternal damnation! Raven winced as yet another vial of liquid on the alchemy trolley exploded sending pinging bits of glass in all directions. Things had seemed to be going quite well until Asha had straddled Blaze, still out cold upon the table.

Then Vervain had turned white. It seemed the copse-man had a crush of sorts on his queen, which at least explained why he'd gone out of his way to help them. However, the Death Warden's discomfort wasn't the issue, but rather Asha now had such a taste for Blaze's blood she'd bitten him and for the last few minutes had been merrily supping from his carotid artery. Their prince was starting to look rather anaemic, and though still comatose, had started fighting back by setting random objects alight. Witness the popping jars and the tome of restoration now merrily smouldering at the corners.

Raven slid back a section of the screening. "I'm going in. I can't leave him."

"Raven!" Sorrow smacked him around the face. "Don't make me sit on you. Relax. Give it time. It'll be okay."

"No, it won't. You can see it's not fucking okay. We're about to lose the only chance we have of seeing more than a glimpse of the cityscape this millennia and he's being drained by a goddamned vampire. That's what you call them, isn't it?" He turned to Vervain. "I remembered. You said it was possible for a human to survive with only one soul, but that you considered them monsters. That's what we've made her into."

"No. It's not the same. Vampires have no Ci'th of their own. Asha's just sensing the link between them. She'll stop soon."

Raven shook his head. She wasn't stopping until she'd drained Blaze of every drop. "I'm going in," he repeated.

"Wait!" Sorrow released his pocket watch from his fist so it dangled on the length of its long silvery chain, prompting a growl of outrage from Raven.

"If you so much as try that thing on me again, I'm going to rip your head off your shoulders."

"No. Not you. I think... I'm not sure..."

"Her? You think it might work on her. Try it. Hell, yeah." Anything was worth a go.

Raven stayed behind the partition, but with the screen pushed back so that an entrance route remained, while Sorrow tiptoed across the Hall of Shadows. He stopped several feet from the table, where he stood with his shoulders hunched so as to seem unthreatening.

"Asha," he coaxed in a sing-song voice. " O' Asha."

If she noticed him, she showed no sign of it at first. Not until he'd padded to within touching distance. Then she looked up from her feasting. A wet ring of blood surrounded her mouth. Slowly, she cocked her head, following Sorrow's cautious movements. Her gaze fastened upon his neck.

In the blink of an eye, Asha was across the table and hurtling towards Sorrow. The impact as she hit him knocked him backwards into the implement trolley, sending it wheeling across the room. Asha crouched low over Sorrow's chest, his arms pinned beneath her knees. She tore open his shirt, exposing his chest and throat.

Raven darted forwards, only for Skaa to catch him and hold him back. "Take care."

Cautiously, Asha sniffed at Sorrow's skin. Her head swayed from side to side, while her clawed hands worked over his breast bone. Sorrow remained rigidly still. Then as quickly as she'd pounced, she backed off with a snarl and returned to Blaze's side.

"Asha?" Sorrow murmured, drawing her attention once more. It was enough. The pendulum had already begun to swing.

Raven, Vervain and Skaa all jostled to get through the door. Raven headed straight for Blaze, leaving Skaa to aid his brother, and Vervain to deal with Asha.

He licked the wound in Blaze's neck and watched in relief as it closed. "I've brought her back to you, Blaze. But I'm not sure how we're going to tame her. Pray its resurrection stress that's making her wild. "The alternative being that they'd created a vile monster that they were going to have to get Blaze to incinerate.

"I've an idea," Skaa said, his long nose back in the smouldering alchemy book. "It might even work. How firmly do you have her, Sorrow? Might a little erotic suggestion work? Raven, slap Blaze around a bit. See if you can get him to open his eyes long enough to draw him into the same spell."

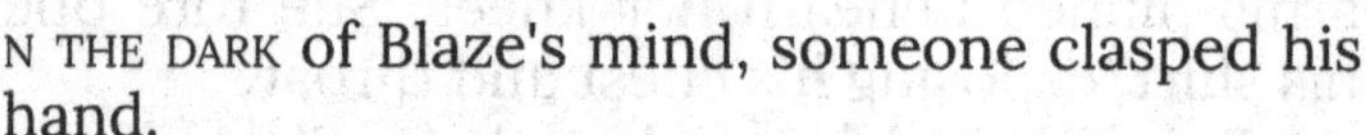

N THE DARK of Blaze's mind, someone clasped his hand.

The cathedral and the burning landscape surrounding it had faded away. Now a second heartbeat thudded alongside his.

Asha—she'd come to him. Her hand stretched out of the darkness, and she held him fast. Her image shimmered before him now, flowing in and out of phase. Slowly the contrast sharpened until he could see her face and not just her outline. She remained impossibly lovely. Her hair stirred gently blown by his breath. A ruddy smear marked the side of her upturned nose and a rosy blush coloured the tops of her cheekbones.

"Where are you? I can't find you." She raised her arms beseechingly.

It struck him as odd to hear her complain of such a thing. His fearless china doll had never once remarked upon the bruises she'd gained in his defence, or the exhaustion he'd driven her to.

But she moaned now, long and hollow, and held herself tight as she shivered.

"Asha, I'm here."

She turned towards his voice, and he saw that her eyes were glazed and unseeing. A void remained were he should have been reflected in her pupils.

"I've marked you, Asha, and I shouldn't have done. It's taken you from me."

"I'm right here," she said, curling her gloved hand around his forearm. "Hush now. Why would I leave?"

"I'm sorry, Asha. I never meant for it to be like this."

Rather embarrassingly, the simple contact between them made his cock stir. That just seemed to confirm his suspicion that youkai weren't known for being overly considerate lovers. Stamina—yeah. Sensitivity—zero. She'd died, for heaven's sakes. Only his libido didn't care.

His lips met hers, butterfly light and every bit as hot as her hands. The gentle pressure left him singed and crying.

Asha stroked away his tears while pressing her lips against his cheek.

From out of the darkness sprang multi-hued flames. His libido spiked again. Blaze shook himself, having realised he'd just nicked her lip with his eye-tooth. The tiny drop of her blood burned inside him all the way to his stomach and poured gasoline on the sexual fire already simmering in his groin.

Blaze returned his attention to the soft plump swell of her lips as they met with his. He cradled her head, holding her lithe curvy body close. There was no masking his erection, so he didn't try. Maybe she understood. Only how could she? She was dead, and yet she was in his arms exactly where she belonged and exactly where he intended to keep her.

The need to possess her grew so strong he didn't pause to question himself before he laid her down and covered her prone form with his body.

Immediately Asha's hands settled upon his bottom, kneading, squeezing and drawing circles. Evidently that wasn't enough, because she wriggled her hands inside his pants.

Skin and skin—so, good. She was warm. And this was what he wanted. No barriers, only the kiss of flesh and the silk of her skin rubbing against him. Yes—and the smell of her hair in his nostrils and her thighs wrapped around his waist.

He'd never yet managed to unlace and divest her of all the layers of her elaborate costume. It became his mission now. Like armour there were knots and buckles to undo, along with hidden layers of padding and secret pockets. He ripped through one seam in his haste. Even here in his head she carried enough weaponry to equip a battalion. He scattered the steel within the ring of fire, along with their clothes. He just couldn't stay clothed around her. It didn't feel right somehow.

Naked, that's how they were meant to be. It's how they best fit together.

"Asha..." He dipped his head and took captive one nipple. While he rolled his tongue around the teat he stroked a hand down to the split of her pussy. She writhed upwards immediately. Blaze drew his thumb along the seam of her lips and she crooned softly against his cheek when he found her pearl. Her back arched, thrusting more of her pert breast towards him. Blaze sucked harder. He released one nipple and gave the other a kiss before shimmying down her body to wet his tongue between her legs.

Man, he could get drunk on the taste of her.

Perhaps he already was.

It wasn't as if what he was doing made any kind of sense.

"Blaze. Swivel around."

He negotiated the turn, supporting the bulk of his weight on his elbows. Hell knows what they were lying on. It shone like black silk, and had the texture of grass. Still, it cushioned his knees as he straddled her head so she could reach his cock.

The touch of her hands still burned, but the same pool of warmth felt magnificent around the head of his shaft. This was how in his ideal world he'd like to wake every day. He'd own a penthouse in the Heights, overlooking acres and acres of manicured lawns and parkways. There'd be a maid and room service and a bed the size of his old bedroom. He'd wake every morning with Asha in his arms, her limbs entangled with his, and they'd make love, slowly, languorously, only rising around noon.

Nice dream. Only the small problem of wings and sharp teeth to negotiate, and the fact she was dead.

So, why did she feel so real? Why did his soul feel complete?

Boy, did the woman know how to suck cock,

concentrating all her efforts on the head, with only the occasional foray down the length of his shaft. Pleasure rose like a storm tide, until it took all of his effort just to hold still.

He had to concentrate on giving to her, too.

Nope, couldn't do it. If he so much as stuck out his tongue...

Asha released him, leaving his over-eager cock begging in free space, while her attention turned to his balls.

"No," he warned. The sensation was sharp and ridiculously sweet.

"No, what?"

"No more. I'll come. I want to be inside you."

"Presumptuous," she scoffed, smacking his arse.

Blaze's hips surged forward seeking any target it could find. Tingling tracks rode up and down his spine. "Asha, please."

"Do you promise to bite me?" she asked.

He gave his head a little shake at the question, afraid he'd somehow misheard. When had her teeth become so sharp?

"If that's what you want."

"Yes, please." She turned so she lay prone beneath him, her head tilted to one side so her throat lay exposed. Black runes circled the stretch of skin above her collarbone and encircled her neck like an elaborate collar. Blaze stared at them. A strange buzzing sensation filled his head, like his brain no longer had enough oxygen. Dry nausea filled his throat. He wasn't sure he wanted to bite. His stomach heaved at the notion of ingesting blood. And yet the lure, the base desire remained.

He sunk into her heat at the same time he bit down. She cried out, but in a welcoming, sort of way.

"I can't." He started panting, head full of angry wasps now.

"You can. I've not tweaked a single feather yet. I want to fly with you."

Feathers—she only had to say it for his wings to appear, soft as snow and black as midnight.

"You're changing," she whispered, her voice impossibly soft. "I like how you feel." She touched the tip of one wing. "They're soft. It makes me want to rub up against you."

"Well, don't. They're sensitive."

"Spoilsport." She ran a finger along the edge of one feather, outright grinning while she did so.

"Concentrate on the blood, Blaze. And the bond."

He really wasn't sure if it was her talking or somebody else.

Already dripping with sweat, Blaze grabbed her hands and locked them together over her head, keeping her pinned there as he summoned every ounce of reserve stamina and drove his hips down fast. At the same time he latched back onto her neck.

Her breath came out too ragged to reply, belly quivering, breasts jumping as he somehow maintained the pace. Fast and furious, it wasn't going to last long, but it sure was good—tidal wave, rocketing through the heavens sort of good.

Asha beat him. He grunted, feeling her muscles ripple. They hugged his shaft. Her breasts thrust up high on the ridge of her ribs, nipples rosy and steepled into crinkled towers. Driving him demented with the need to latch on. He couldn't quite get them in his mouth and maintain the punishing pace. Besides, the blood in his mouth tasted impossibly sweet.

Somehow she freed a hand from his grip and went straight for his wings. She touched him thrice in total. That's all it took to push him over the precipice. One moment he was just about hanging on. The next his orgasm squeezed from him in jets, over and over, until he flopped down sated and wrung dry, his limbs quivering and boneless.

"I love you," she whispered, pressing her lips right up close to his ear.

This time he didn't hold back from saying it, too. He wanted her to know it was mutual.

A STREAK OF blood lay across the right side of her breast when he eventually summoned enough energy to roll off her and onto the weirdly silky black grass. It wasn't grass. It was a tablecloth, and he fell further than he expected, landing on his knees on a marble tiled floor. Worse than the immediate crippling pain in his knees was the realisation he was buck naked, wrapped in steel fishing twine, and his elite guard and Vervain were all staring at him as though he'd grown an extra head.

"Oh, fuck!" he murmured. He tentatively pushed himself onto his feet, inwardly cringing in realisation of what he'd just done. Sure enough

Asha lay upon the table, her clothes rumpled and smeared with blood.

This was bad. It was really fucking bad.

Blaze clapped his hands to his head. Bad. Bad. Bad. He didn't want to think about it in any more detail than that. She was dead, for heaven's sake.

A soft caress brushed across his abs. He looked down at the table again. Asha stared back at him. Her eyes were open and clear as diamonds. She sat, a faint smile creasing the corners of her lips, and tugged the train of the dress she'd been laid out in around her exposed breasts.

"Asha! Wha—How is this possible?"

Before he had time for any more questions, her lips met his, drawing him into an intense kiss that immediately poured fuel on all the smouldering embers of his earlier passion.

"Asha." His hand slid through her hair to the back of her neck and he kissed her again. "I thought I'd lost you forever, but you were still part of me. The link still remained. I couldn't make sense of it."

The smile upon her lips broadened, exposing newly sharpened teeth, and Blaze's hand strayed involuntarily to his neck as he recalled the first of his dreams. Flakes of dried blood clung to his fingers when he withdrew them. It had been no simple vision but a genuine moment of connection.

"How?" He glanced up at his guards.

As one they shrugged.

"Just a little bit of alchemical tomfoolery. Nothing much." Raven whistled.

Skaa slunk off into a corner, while his brother

put on a pair of darkened penny-shades. Only Vervain met his gaze.

"Blaze. There are rules to this triumvirate. The link isn't as infallible as it would normally be. You'll have to work at maintaining the link."

"And work hard at it," Skaa muttered from over in the corner.

"Meaning what?"

Damn, he couldn't get over seeing her sitting there beside him, living, breathing... He kissed her again for good measure. Whatever he had to do to maintain the link he'd do it, no matter how gristly or arduous the task.

"I want to make Talon pay," she said.

"Agreed," he promised. First, he needed a moment to appreciate the miracle that Vervain and the others had accomplished. And he needed to thank them. He wanted to celebrate her return, not immediately lapse back into strife. He picked Asha up and spun her around in his arms until he was giddy with joy and dizzy and her laughter filled the room and his heart. Only when he saw Vervain's scowl did he subdue his mirth.

"Sorry, what did you say?" he apologised, assuming the Death Warden's annoyance stemmed from his inattentiveness. The fact his lips remained thinned alerted him to Vervain's deeper concerns. Only then did he spy the ring of sigils drawn around Asha's neck. He lowered her gingerly. Just how fragile was she? She'd always been so strong and robust. Would she even tolerate being treated like the china doll she so resembled? And yet, in his mind he relieved the horror of her death and knew he had to keep her safe.

Her eyes saddened as his mood darkened. Raven stepped alongside them, placing an arm around each of their shoulders.

"Welcome back, both of you." His warm smile relieved some of the tension from Blaze's jaw. "In essence what Vervain was saying is that you have to behave like a good little demon, Blaze. No more of this pussyfooting around pretending to be human. You need to up the kink and develop a major fetish for the red stuff. Is that about it?" He sought askance of Vervain, who nodded in response to his question.

"So, I have to nurture a taste for drinking blood?"

Weirdly the thought no longer totally disgusted him. Maybe his instincts were returning, if not his memories of the past. Then again, maybe it was simply an awareness and acceptance of what he was.

"More like sharing it," Raven corrected, "and you need to be rigorous about it because... Well, let's just say I'm not setting foot in the Death Ward again. Ever. Not even for you. Much as I love you."

Asha shuffled out of Raven's grip. He guessed old tensions didn't dissolve overnight. They eyed one another warily, until Asha backed down and began to wind the long train of her dress around her body.

"You owe Jaku your life," Vervain remarked to her. "I don't know how much you remember."

"It's cloudy," she mumbled, clearly uncomfortable pursuing that line of conversation.

"Why?" Blaze cautiously asked. What had

Asha's ex-partner done? He recalled Jaku had tried to intervene at the meeting with Talon, and that afterwards he'd been told they'd brought him back to the castle to pry for information. At the time he hadn't cared. Had Jaku provided them with an advantage? "I think one of you had better explain what's been going on in detail. In what way does Asha owe him? What bargains have been struck in my absence?"

"You both owe him. Jaku travelled with us to the Death Ward," Vervain began, only for his words to peter out as his throat became choked with emotion. He shook his head and tugged up the cowl of his robe so his face dissolved into shadows. Blaze turned to Raven. His chief guard initially shook his head, but then perched on the edge of the table and took up the tale.

"So the Thirteen Princes accepted a straight exchange of my Ti soul for Jaku's?" Asha queried after the explanation was done. "Why did they ask for so little?"

"They had wanted Jaku for some time," Vervain replied. A whole paragraph of silent conversation seemed to take place between Asha and Vervain, the subtleties of which were lost on Blaze, but he shared Asha's emotional response as if it were his own.

The closeness of the connection came as something of a shock. In the past it had been a simple awareness of her emotional state, like a gentle tug upon his senses. Now the acute pain of her loss and her gratitude struck him deeply. He and Asha were together now, only because Jaku had made that sacrifice. The fact that there'd been no love lost between him and Jaku made his sacrifice all the more poignant.

"We will all honour him," he announced. There was no question of that.

The proclamation brightened both Vervain and Asha's faces.

"We'll obey you in all things of course," Skaa stepped forward, "but before we become side-tracked—"

Blaze shushed him into silence. "We'll honour him once the moon no longer conspires against us. You were about to tell me that the Blood Moon has risen, were you not?"

"I was." Skaa gave a stiff bow. "My apologies, but now is the time for decisive action, not citing eulogies to the dead. Our spies report increasing activity in and around the cathedral. Talon is up to something. A something likely targeted at you."

"Then what do you suggest, my advisors?" Blaze looked around for a chair, and some clothing. He soon gave up and sat on the floor, whereupon he pulled Asha onto his knee. He'd like nothing better than to sink into a warm pool of water with her and soap away all their cares, but that luxury would have to wait. The battle could no longer be avoided.

Sorrow, Skaa, and Raven huddled around him. Vervain, not an official part of his guard, lingered on the fringe of the group.

Sorrow began. "A direct attack upon the cathedral is likely to cause the least number of civilian casualties. That's been your stated concern all along. Additionally, I don't think Talon anticipates such a direct assault. He doesn't see you as a genuine threat, more as an inconvenience to be disposed of."

"That," Asha remarked, "is how he sees everyone. People are there to be exploited and once their use has passed..." She grimaced. None of them needed further elaboration. They'd all seen the results first hand. "The assault needs to be hard and swift. Any sort of extended siege will only rally support for Talon. He and his hunters may be feared, but they are still ostensibly seen as protectors, whereas you are monsters. Anything you do will be viewed in the worst possible light. Talon rule, not demon rule. That's the slogan he's been touting about to anyone with half an ear to listen."

"Let us not forget also that he is also something more akin to us now. He's winged and likely more robust," Raven said.

Vervain gave a deep sigh at this assessment. "Talon cannot truly be described as having been human for the longest time. Like Blaze, you should consider him unique. He is neither human nor demon, but something different again, which I hasten to add also means the outcome of this battle you intend to wage is by no means certain. Either one of you might fulfil the prophecy. Consider also that it is you, not Talon presently causing such hardship to the townsfolk. The fires you created have already consumed the warehouse district, much of the jewellery quarter, and a portion of the Birdcage. Likely enough without rain, the fires will soon cross the canal."

Blaze stared at him in mute shock. Then still naked he ran to the balcony and looked up at the city. Few lights penetrated the thick ash clouds. He could discern little of what was occurring. "The people though. They are fine?"

"They are hungry and homeless and cold. I do not think they will welcome your arrival."

"But nor will they turn to Talon out of choice." Poised and stately in her newly constructed dress, Asha joined Blaze upon the balcony. "Not after the massacre on Hangover Street. The people mistrust him. The youkai are an easy target, but even now with the castle floating up here in the sky, I wonder how many of them truly believe you exist."

Blaze bristled at the notion, but acknowledged what she said was true. Despite the ubiquitous presence of the Talon for many, many decades, most of the population didn't actually believe the youkai existed. Maybe a few of them had changed their minds now, but probably not. It suited their narrow world view to run around with blinkers on.

He took Asha by the hands. "I want you to know that this battle isn't my desire. I never wanted this throne. However, I've an obligation. I made a promise. If they helped me free you from Talon's grasp..."

"I want revenge," she spat back, before raking her teeth over her bottom lip. "Do what you will to Talon. It's not as if he cares for anyone but himself. If he rules, he'll be a tyrant. People will live and die according to his whims. When he promises them a human paradise, he means to give them the world as he desires it. Only those with strong stomachs and a similar bent for sadism will rejoice over having him as a leader."

"Then you'll walk at my side?" To Blaze's utter shock, she shook her head. His stared at her open jawed, with his heart flip-flopping inside his chest. "But?"

"You need a way inside, my love. I intend to call ahead." Her smile ran all the way to her eyes, defied logic with its malicious beauty.

"Be my queen," he asked. He wanted her with all his heart.

She laughed and darted out of his grasp when he reached for her. "If all goes well tonight, then ask me again. Now where are my weapons?"

They were soon brought to her along with fresh clothing. Blaze also dressed. "Where? Where will you go?"

"To the cathedral, of course."

In horror he watched her grow more insubstantial the further she moved from his side, until he could see straight through her. "Trust me, Blaze. Listen for my signal. I know a way in." He blinked and she vanished altogether. Only a tiny spatter of red dust remained on the floor where she'd stood.

"Damn." He would have to trust in the link between them to warn him of imminent danger she faced. And pray that she knew what she was doing. "Time to rally the troops."

Raven launched into action. "I think we can be ready in fifteen minutes."

"Good. No, wait. If we all go, there'll be too much blood shed. Just us, and the rest of my elite guard."

"Blaze."

"Have them prepare, but hold back until they're sent word. We'll go in first. This is about combating Talon's evil, not subjugating the townsfolk to my will. Seriously, Raven, if anyone objects have them drafted in for larvae herding duty. Things have gotten out of hand around here. It's impractical to run the gauntlet every time you want to take a nap or change your clothes. Speaking of which, I want some armour."

9. BLOOD MOON

**

"When the Blood Moon rises, the demons' prince will wake
from his thousand-year slumber and cast a shadow across the sun.
The city will become a youkai paradise, a vast playground of
perversity and vice. However, his rebirth will
encompass many stages, during which time we
will know him only by his mark."
--Kell's Prophecy from the Apostle's Dialogue.

**

"THERE IS ONE thing, before we go marching off to war," Sorrow remarked, as they warily climbed the stairs to the turret that purportedly held Blaze's armour. It lay just above his bedchamber and this section of the palace was eerily quiet. Every word echoed into infinity, or at least into the black void at the base of the winding stairwell.

Blaze especially, expected larvae to burst through every crack in the severely worn steps. While the concept of encasing himself in metal or leather plates seemed rather mediaeval, considering his recent close encounters with clawed and psychotic knife wielding maniacs he didn't fancy taking chances. If nothing else, it would hopefully help keep him upright long enough to get past all of Talon's dolls and to the man himself.

"What is it?" He continued to power up the

spiral steps, not really paying attention to Sorrow's tone. He needed to get out of the palace and over to the cathedral, so that he could back up Asha pronto.

On the landing Sorrow skipped ahead. "It's about Grace and Florian."

"What about them?"

Sorrow pressed a palm to Blaze's chest, bringing him to an abrupt and unwelcome halt. "You're tweaking my tail feathers, right?"

"Nope." Blaze shook his head for emphasis. The last time he recalled seeing either of them was as they were leaving to attend that stitch up with Talon. Actually—he screwed his eyes up tight—the tiniest mental fragment of a further encounter hung on the edge of his consciousness, but, nope, he couldn't recall it.

"No way, Blaze. I realise that they're a pair of insensitive, offensive idiots, but what you did was a bit much, and we really need all our strength at the moment."

Having determined from the remark that Sorrow wasn't about to let up or budge from his current position blocking the stairs, Blaze took the opportunity to catch his breath. This landing was about sixty times worse than the previous one. Never mind larvae, there were about four hundred different types of moss growing in the cracks, some of them with eyes.

"If I had any idea what you were talking about."

"You're serious? You don't remember. You're not just still pissed off with them?"

"I don't actually recall being pissed off with them, leastways not genuinely pissed off. They're both a bit annoying but..." He shrugged. "I haven't put them on a hit list."

Sorrow's face showed absolute horror. He blinked at Blaze several times, while his mouth hung open. "You fried them! You melted them into one...being...thing."

"I did not."

"You fucking well did. Tell him, Raven."

Raven, who had been playing rear guard, stuck his arm out to steady himself against the wall. Blaze watched revolted as the mossy eye stalks strained towards his hand.

"Hey geroff," he grumbled as they curled around his fingers. "If we're talking Grace and Florian, yeah you did, Blaze, and it ain't pretty. Hadn't mentioned it because I'm guessing you haven't a clue how to undo it. And hey, I didn't want to spoil the happy reunion moment." He stuck his chin out and grimaced at Sorrow. "The best we can hope for is splitting them down the middle and hoping it results in something functional. We'll call in a surgeon to take a look later. Either way, they're fuck all use to us at the moment, so there's no point dwelling on it. Right?" He knocked Sorrow's arm out of the way, allowing Blaze to resume his climb.

"Why'd you have to bring that up now?" Blaze barely heard Raven's softly spoken growl, but by the time the words had bounced off the walls a few time, they may as well have been shouted.

Blaze glanced back at the pair of them locking horns. "Hey. Get me into this armour and then show me." Forward motion, that's what they needed, not endless delays.

HIS ARMOUR COMPRISED of a body suit that zipped on beneath his clothing made of some sort of metallic mesh, breathable, but about as sexy as a pair of long johns. The outer layer consisted of numerous leather plates that buckled together, a cape, and enough boot to support an entire ecosystem. Blaze peered dubiously into its depths; something was scuttling around in the bottom. He dropped it and kicked the boot into the corner.

"Forget it. I'll stick to the leathers and my jacket." The outfit had served him well so far, and it was pretty universal wear for the various street gangs that operated out of the Birdcage. "The only thing that get-up is going to inspire is laughter."

"Here." Raven threw him a piece of moulded inch thick leather, which turned out to be a shoulder piece. "That do ya?"

Sorrow helped Blaze strap it on over the top of his jacket.

"I can see a new craze starting." Raven gave a nod of approval. "Wait and see. Everyone will be wearing them."

"Fat lot of good it'll be if he gets stabbed in the guts," Sorrow griped. His mouth set into a rigid thin line, but whatever else he'd thought of saying, he kept to himself. Blaze realised Raven's right eye was burning. He didn't want to know what Raven was seeing, but regardless of how lopsided that shoulder plate made him feel, it was staying on.

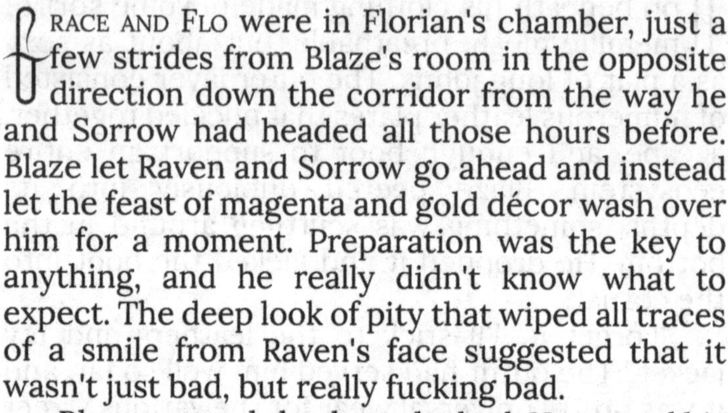

GRACE AND FLO were in Florian's chamber, just a few strides from Blaze's room in the opposite direction down the corridor from the way he and Sorrow had headed all those hours before. Blaze let Raven and Sorrow go ahead and instead let the feast of magenta and gold décor wash over him for a moment. Preparation was the key to anything, and he really didn't know what to expect. The deep look of pity that wiped all traces of a smile from Raven's face suggested that it wasn't just bad, but really fucking bad.

Blaze crossed slowly to the bed. He turned his head away immediately, hand clasped across his mouth as he choked back the wave of nausea that threatened to purge his guts.

Truthfully, he couldn't see them as a pair anymore. They were melted like wax and twisted together to form a two-headed, multi-limbed amorphous mass. He'd turned them into the sort of monster that chased you through empty streets in your most horrific nightmares. Not that this particular rotund ball of limbs could walk. Nor, he realised, could it talk, or do anything else. Perhaps, blessedly so, because surely any voice it had would be used only to scream at the cruelty and agony of its condition.

"I did this," he croaked, hardly sounding the last syllable. If he had, then he had to correct it. He couldn't walk away. Only how? What had he done to make them like this in the first place?

Blaze choked back a sob. He'd become a

monster. And yet, everything he'd accomplished so far had been done on instinct or prompted by panic. He had no idea how to genuinely command the power at his disposal. Separating brother and sister would take a level of skill that far surpassed his abilities. But he had to try, just like he was going to have to try and beat Talon, an alchemist with years of experience to his name and an uncanny ability to bend and twist words to best suit his needs.

Well, this was going to be the sharpest learning curve he'd ever faced.

Blaze closed his eyes and pictured the pair as best he could. The mental construct was blurry at best. He'd spent mere moments in their presence, Florian particularly. In fact, his overriding impression of the male demon was that he was tall, blond, and had a taste for coxcombs. Facial details were sketchy and he had to ask Raven and Sorrow to fill in some blanks over his physique.

He had slightly more to go on with Grace. Her choice of outfits left little to the imagination, plus there'd been that feverish episode with Raven she'd somehow become part of. Her image was definitely sharper.

So, that was his goal set, which just left the actual unravelling to contend with.

First he divided the amorphous blob into nice easy mental sections. Then slowly, as if holding a large lump of clay, he began to reshape.

If he rotated a certain limb this way and applied pressure here, and then twisted and... He worked on, steadily unravelling their bodies from one another, severing parts that simply didn't belong until he saw them separate and whole again. Only then did he allow his knees to sag, whereupon he collapsed to the floor.

"Are they?" he murmured.

Raven's firm grip tightened around his shoulder. "You did it, Blaze. They're whole. Correct number of arms and legs, a head on each body and no random extras. Leastways, none I can see."

"But they're not as they were." He knew that without seeing them. Something about the process had changed them. Gingerly, Blaze raised his eyelids and looked over his work. Two pairs of deep-set mahogany eyes peered back at him. He expected a backlash, screams of outrage and accusation, but the two youkai—they looked far more similar than before—remained discouragingly quiet.

"Grace, Florian?" Sorrow reached out to touch them both. "You can talk, right? You're fine now?"

No one blinked. A significant pause stretched on, making Blaze's ears throb with its silence.

"Of what would you wish us to speak?" Florian eventually replied.

Blaze breathed a sigh of relief. "I'd like to know you're all right. I'd also like to extend you an apology for my abysmal temper and lack of control. The crime hardly warranted such a punishment."

Florian cocked his head as if desperately trying to understand what was being said. Grace chattered her teeth, which were now narrow and needle-sharp. "We're no longer whole," she whimpered, her voice full of despair. "What have you done? You've torn us asunder. Return us to how we were."

It took Blaze a moment to realise she wanted to be that blob again, not her former snake-like self. "Why? Why would you want to be like that?"

"We were one," they replied in unison.

One? Oh! He'd wanted them to understand the connection, the despair he'd felt over losing Asha. He remembered now, the fire, their rudeness.

"But you couldn't...well, do anything." Raven scratched his head in incomprehension. The pair ignored him. Their eager gazes remained fixed expectantly upon Blaze, who shrugged. Right now he needed fighters. He wasn't about to roll them together again. Okay, he wasn't about to do that to them again anyway, no matter now nicely they pleaded. "Later, I'll work on it. Right now there's a battle to wage."

"You wish us to fight apart?"

"That's right. If you're able," he replied.

"You know, actually Blaze," Raven butted in. "I'm not sure if that's wise." The pilot light at the heart of his pupil had flared again, and burned with a lilac flame as his gaze skittered over Florian to reach Grace. "You're tough. I'll give you that, but you're no warrior."

Surprisingly, given their current closeness, Florian backed him up. "It's true. Grace, it would be best if you didn't fight."

"Don't leave me." Bright tears filled her eyes, and her brother reached out to her.

"Never, my love. Never. I'll carry you here." Florian pressed her cheek tight to his chest. A faint golden glow began to spread and entwine them. Blaze watched it creep over their skin. His hand stretched towards it without a thought for his safety. He pulled back at the last moment, and watched the siblings shift form, adopting youkai characteristics in place of their human guises. But rather than change completely, they each grew only a single wing, and only one side of their bodies transformed.

Florian and Grace faced one another with their palms pressed together. The magic flowed back and forth between them, pulsing, expanding, and then following an exchange of nods, the glow gradually consumed Grace entirely, reducing her to a ball of pure energy that pierced Florian's chest.

He staggered backwards.

Raven caught him. "Okay?"

After a pause, in which his face contorted into a look of pure agony, Florian smiled. "Never better, thank you." Having regained his balance, he flexed his newly paired wings.

"Grace?" Blaze whispered. He hardly dared ask.

"Is sleeping." Florian clasped one hand to his chest where the ball of energy had pierced him. "She's safe in here."

It seemed the pair had discovered a way to become one again without his help.

"Then let's go."

ASHA UNRAVELLED HERSELF from the mist in the quiet of the Chapel of Nine Altars, the former heart of the cathedral. The dust lay undisturbed on the floor and inches thick. There were no candles lit. Few, if any, of the demon hunters that called the cathedral home ventured this far beyond the choir stalls to the ambulatory where the old saints held court. The crossing had become the new hub of activity and the plateau from which Talon ruled. The trace whisper of activity flowed in from that direction.

She stopped to gaze upon Kell's humble shrine. Of all the long forgotten apostles, only his words had impacted upon her life. Kell's Prophecy—the forgotten chapter—torn from the Apostle's dialogue out of fear, dismissed and banished, like the youkai of which he spoke. Both were faerie tales and both had come back to haunt them.

Of course, the church itself had collapsed two centuries ago, rejected en mass by the people who no longer believed in heaven or hell. How could they, when the dead walked abroad each night?

The exact date of Talon's occupation hadn't been recorded, or if it had, the transcription remained with him. Perhaps, he'd even played a part in nudging out the former arch-bishop. She'd never asked Talon his age, but his memory stretched back a long way and he looked the same now as he had the day she'd first met him.

That bastard had killed her. She'd known he would eventually, although she hadn't anticipated such a direct assault.

Revenging her death would be bittersweet.

She understood Blaze's pain, and his need to strike back, but Talon was hers. Violence was part of her nature, not so for Blaze. He wasn't inured to it in the way she was. Besides, she'd never once waited for a man to save her. She wasn't about to start now.

All the windows at this end of the building were stained. Asha lingered in a pool of moonlight. Nineteen and hopelessly naïve she'd stood in this forgotten quarter of the cathedral and thought herself saved. She'd been incredibly foolish in the early days, failing to see beyond the surface to the dark heart of the order. Of course it hadn't taken long to wise up. But by then, it was too late. Talon had noticed her, and so began years of torture.

Really she ought to have seen him for what he was sooner and got out instead of making constant excuses. Blaze had changed that. He'd given her a reason to go. Prior to that there'd been no real incentive. What was out there for her among the general populace besides that which she'd sought to escape in the first place? The thought of relinquishing her sword in favour of a homemaker's apron gave her heart palpitations. Domesticity and babies had never been on her agenda. That hadn't changed, regardless of how tightly she was bound to Blaze. She hoped by acting independently of his plans he realised that.

Not that she intended to abandon him. Heavens no. Blaze needed someone to steer him right. He indulged his emotions too much. He was impulsive and contrary. It would take time for him to mature. Meanwhile, she had no intention of letting any of those demons manipulate him. She'd hold him to the promises he'd made—symbiosis, not slavery for the human populace. They weren't to become second class citizens. She wouldn't tolerate a youkai occupation.

She was getting ahead of herself though. Talon first. Consequences later.

Staying in the shadows, Asha left the ambulatory and crossed the choir stalls. The only hymns that were sung here now were pleas to that devil—Talon.

She wondered if he sensed her presence as she sensed his.

His image was burned into her mind's eye. If he wasn't directing his troops from his throne-like chair, then the most likely place she'd find him would be in the former chapter house.

How little they all knew, these former companions of hers. She realised it when she passed several of them in the cloisters and they responded to her presence with a conventional nod. Were they not aware of her death? Time had passed oddly these past few days, so that she wasn't certain how long she'd been gone.

Blind cattle marked for slaughter. Did they even know why they were fighting? Didn't they realise Blaze wasn't the primary threat, or that they were being led by the biggest demon of them all?

The door to Talon's chambers stood closed. Asha seeped beneath it, rising on the inside as a column of mist, before slowly resuming her shape. Being mostly spirit certainly had some advantages. Oh, she was solid enough to the touch, but she didn't have to be, and being able to travel as part of the air certainly made accessing places she wasn't invited a whole lot easier.

No point attempting to pick Talon's locks. He issued instructions straight to the wood.

Talon's room stood empty. The bed lay unmade.

Standards were slipping.

Asha crossed to the table that housed Talon's alchemical equipment and dragged it away from the wall, wincing over the noise of the vials she jostled. One fell and shattered, slopping acid or worse onto the floor. It fizzed and gnawed at the polished wooden boards. Asha threw a rag over the puddle.

One of these panels—she searched the carved wainscoting with her bare fingertips, seeking out that one tiny imperfection in the grain.

Talon didn't use the tunnel. Not to her knowledge, anyway. Maybe he knew about it, maybe he didn't. She'd learned of it from Vervain. He from a book. He'd told her of it one night when she'd gone to him bleeding and sore unable to find Jaku. He'd meant it as an escape route, hadn't realised it was accessed from the heart of Talon's domain.

Finally she found the catch, barely more than a pinprick in the wood, into which she stabbed a hairgrip. The mechanism released with a click causing the oak panel to swing outwards.

Asha snatched up one of the blue orbs Talon used to light his chamber, blew on it to light it, and then slid into the gloom of the former bishop's garderobe.

Pewter and china crockery stood stacked against one wall. Dusty vestments hung on rotten hangers against the other. She snagged her foot on a tattered ermine, provoking a series of squeaks. Mice scampered around her feet. They bolted when she lowered the light.

Talon had clearly never walked here. He'd have stripped away the assets and exterminated the vermin. That was his favourite hobby after all. Well, second favourite after tormenting her. Alternatively, he'd have hidden something of value here, and since all she could see was dust that seemed unlikely. Talon liked to admire what he owned. He'd never have resisted the urge to take regular peeks.

To the right of the L-shaped chamber a squat doorway led into a narrow corridor, fashioned inside what she presumed were the cathedral walls. Holding the light so as not to blind herself, she hurried along. Time was short. She might not have violated the main chamber door, but there were other wards on his room that would have alerted Talon to an intrusion.

It wasn't long before the muggy air became fresher. She began a slow trek down a treacherous stair, which surely plunged down below the level of the plaza. Vervain maintained the passage ended in the vicinity of the quayside.

He was right, too. The swampy stench of the canal wafted to her from under a stout iron door at the end of a further passageway. Five bolts barred her exit, each rusted into place and more difficult than the last to wiggle open. Things would have been so much simpler if she could have seeped beneath it like the previous door, but she needed this route open for Blaze.

Her fingers were stained and sore by the time

she'd freed the last bolt. Beyond lay a storage room stacked with barrels and beyond that a platform directly onto the quayside, with steps up to the plaza.

Out here the stench of burning timbers poisoned the air, obliterating the normal pong of the water. White flakes danced in the air and formed a grey foam where the canal met the retaining wall. Part of the Birdcage was still alight. The eyrie was lit up like a beacon. For several moments she watched men and women run past carrying buckets and enormous billhooks. They were tearing down the wooden houses, trying to stop the spreading flames.

Blaze—Blaze had done this.

Asha slumped against the soot stained wall of the canal. She had to trust him and at least give him a chance to make things right.

Befriend a demon and you're wasted. Trust a demon and you're dead meat. Love a demon and you're a laughingstock. Talon's doctrine ran through her head. Had she become all those things? Yet, Blaze had given her many more reasons to trust him than Talon ever had. And the youkai had help restore her to life, regardless of their reasons.

She closed her eyes and concentrated on the main image of Blaze she held in her mind. It was as she'd first seen him. Blond hair combed into gravity defying spikes and a leather jacket fringed in crow's feathers slung around his back, but hanging open to reveal the tight black T-shirt he wore beneath.

She heard the drumming of his heart.

The moment Blaze sensed her, warmth

flooded her pleasure centres. Eschewing words, she passed him an image of the entry route into the cathedral.

Asha didn't wait. She tracked straight back to Talon's chamber. Blaze could help subdue the rest of the order, but Talon was hers.

ALON STOOD WAITING for her in his chamber. Well, perhaps not specifically waiting for her, but for whoever the intruder was. He didn't cower when he saw her, only eyed her suspiciously.

"Have you come back to haunt me?" A rude smile played upon his lips. "You never could resist my charm." He inclined his head to one side, gazed at her clearly fascinated. "Isn't it a little early in the day for the Ghost Wind to be abroad in the City? Although, I suppose you could be forgiven for thinking it's dusk considering all the ash in the sky blocking out the sun. Your friend Blaze is responsible. Were you aware of that?"

He blinked at her slowly, and his eyes grew intensely blue. "Of course you're not obligated to him anymore, but what of the Old Princes? Are they too out to stake their claim upon the city tonight?"

"I'm not dead, Talon. You didn't quite manage it." She raised a gloved hand to her neck and traced her fingertips over the raised stitches and rows of runes burned into her flesh. For a moment, it seemed it a shame she was no longer a savage, rage-filled, disembodied head. Sucking the marrow from his bones would have made a sweet form of vengeance indeed.

Swiftly, she released her sword from its sheath.

"You're not entirely living either," Talon remarked. "Has he enslaved you even in death? I freed you, Asha. I gave you the means of escape."

She stepped around the cock-eyed table, ensuring she had space to swing. Maybe she'd take his head, just so he knew exactly how it felt. She didn't suppose it would actually kill him. He'd probably just re-grow a new one, like the damn reptile he was.

"You murdered me in cold blood because it suited your purposes, so don't try and fob me off with a yarn about doing it out of love. All you hoped was that you would cripple Blaze. Only it didn't. It made him stronger. He's stronger than ever, now. And he's coming for you, Talon."

"Thank you most graciously for the warning." Talon fell back a pace or two, placing the foot of the bed between them. "So he desires revenge, does he? What for exactly? It's not as if I actually took you from him. Oh no, in fact I seem to have witnessed your marriage. It should be me hunting him down. I'm the damaged party after all. You were my lover."

"Don't pretend this is about me. You want his crown. Nothing else. All this—" She swept her sword arm wide to indicate their surroundings and all that she'd been part of. "—it's all just lies. One built upon another. I swore to defend and protect, but against what? The youkai menace never really existed. How many more have we killed on suspicion that the youkai have preyed upon in all that time? How many murders have actually been attributed to demons in the last century? Five? Six, maybe?" She shook her head again at Talon's continued silence. "Not even that. You've been using fear to keep people in line."

Talon pulled back his shoulders and stood tall. A crafty smile lit his face and bled into the luminous blue of his cat-like eyes. He took a pace back towards her, so that he stood in range of her sword.

"You know the truth of the records, Asha. I won't debate them with you. And you've seen what a sex-starved demon can do. Those half-chewed victims weren't make-believe. Your lover's a monster. Best not forget it."

"Well, I seem to have a thing for monsters."

He laughed—a deep down genuine rumble of delight.

"Oh, Asha. You flatterer." He sobered equally fast, all trace of amusement fleeing his face. "What I'd really like to know is if you genuinely trust him. You don't, do you? You don't believe he's the strength or fortitude to hold all those bloodthirsty demons in check. Forget the last few days. Think about what you know of the youkai and what you know of Blaze. He's a boy, Asha. A lonely little boy, who thinks that wearing crow feathers and ringing his eyes with kohl make him cool. The youkai may have sworn loyalty to his face, but they'll run riot behind his back once they are established down here. He's a puppet king, destined to be replaced."

"Singe your wings, did he, the last time you had to run away?"

Talon folded his arms across his chest. She

was so accustomed to seeing him half-clad that his near nakedness had barely registered. The top of his trousers hung ludicrously low on his hips. He'd added a new rune onto the left side of his stomach, the silvered lines of which briefly dazzled her. One of these days he was going to run out of skin to deface.

"What has he promised you that's bought so much loyalty?"

"To let the humans remain free," she responded automatically.

A second wave of laughter rumbled in Talon's throat. "That's good. That's a really good one. He'll promise. He may even try to keep his word, but watch and see, Asha. He'll never truly act to stop the indiscretions once they occur. Humans are food to them, nothing more. Well—food and a thing with which to appease their appetite for kinky sex."

"Shut up!" She swung the sword at him, forcing him to dance backwards. "You know nothing of him. He's lived centuries longer than you."

"You silly fool. I know everything about him. Far more than he remembers. Who do you think thrust you into his path? I orchestrated it."

She froze, stunned. How could that be?

"Liar."

He shook his head. "It's all going perfectly to plan, Asha. Did you never think it strange that you're the only female member of the order?"

No—he was playing on her fears, trying to manipulate her in order to get himself out of a tight spot. He knew she'd come for revenge. She jabbed at him again.

"I didn't recruit you just to get inside your knickers."

"Stop it! Just stop it. You can't even be truthful about what you are." This time she swung meaning to hit.

Talon moved impossibly fast. Not away, but towards her. Right in tight against her body, so that his loins pressed firm against her hip. Impossibly strong hands closed around her wrist and shook the sword from her grip.

"And what am I, Asha? No more or less human than you. We've both outlived our allotted time spans. Neither of us cared to give up. The methods may be different but the net results are the same."

"We're nothing alike."

She said it, but deep down she wept over how similar aspects of their personalities were. They were both fighters, survivors. They both thrived on challenge and the prospect of pain. There'd been times when those two things were all that had sustained her, when she'd longed for pain because only it could penetrate the numb void in which she lived.

Had she been numb before she'd joined the Talon, or had Talon purged her of her emotions?

Blaze had made her feel again.

Talon jerked her fingertips up towards his lips, and ripped the glove from her hand.

Asha pulled away from him, but he held her fast. "Don't touch me."

He traced the contours of the sigil burned into her palm with his tongue, which made her whole hand burn, then he sucked her thumb into his mouth.

Her sword lay upon the floor, but she had more than one weapon to her name. One lightning fast sweep, that's all it would take. Straight into his stomach. Let him try and concentrate on world domination while trying to keep his guts intact.

Yet something held her back. What if, said a tiny voice inside her head. What if this were all part of some elaborate plan? They'd all presumed Talon merely wanted to strip Blaze of his crown and take outright control of the Old City, but what if his scheming were directed at accomplishing something bigger than that?

"I said, let go." She drew the dagger with her off hand, and pressed the point into his skin just a fraction below his navel.

"Let me see those runes." Ignoring the dagger, he ripped aside the fabric covering her throat. "Vervain, again. That Death Warden and I really ought to have words."

A low rumble like distant thunder sounded from outside, followed by a series of whistles and thud that shook the buildings foundations. The floor vibrated beneath her feet, and sent a shock wave right up her shins. Asha swayed, despite the hard press of Talon's body against her. A second thud caused the floor to ripple, and every piece of glass wear on the table, save four small jars, to smash.

"What in hell?" Their words echoed one another.

Asha's sight blurred. It took her a moment to realise she was seeing Blaze's field of vision overlaid with hers. He was outside on the plaza, shooting Talon's own glass cannonballs right at the cathedral. Flames licked up the outer walls, and entwined the crenulations. One of the stained windows overlooking the transept shattered, leaving behind an array of jagged glass teeth.

The vision faded as Talon's fingers curled around her throat. He dug his nails into her barely mended scars. Asha wrapped her hand around his balls, squeezed until tears appeared in his eyes. His jaw locked tight against the scream brewing in his throat.

"I could take your head again," he growled into her ear. "Let go."

She twisted her wrist instead. Maybe that hadn't been so wise. Sure, he screamed, but it also melted away the last of his patience, or love, or whatever it was he had for her. He shoved her hard enough to send her sprawling across the bed. For one awful moment she anticipated him coming towards her meaning to possess her again. That simply couldn't happen. She would never lie still and be his again. Asha rolled gaining her feet on the far side of the bed. He didn't pounce. He didn't even scramble toward her. Still dancing in agony and cradling his hurts with one hand, he rummaged through the mess of flasks scattered over the table tops.

"Yes!" He turned to face her, popping the cork off a sickly green liquid. From out of the mask of pain, he found a smile. "There are uncertainties in every plan, so I hope you'll understand if I make my exit with a little bargaining chip in hand." He threw the contents of the flask at her. She backstepped, but gobs of the liquid splashed her face and seeped through the weft of her clothing.

Chilly fluid dribbled onto her neck. She wiped it away, but wherever it touched her skin became cold. Winter seeped into her veins, numbing everything, stopping her heart, even as it sped in fear.

"There's no point in trying to go all misty on me. I can't have you running off now, can I?" Talon staggered toward her, the key that hung around his neck lifted on the extent of its chain. He tapped the metal teeth twice to her forehead. "Sweet dreams, my love."

10: BLAZE

**

"We will know him by his mark,
and both youkai and bleeders will fall down before his gaze."
–Kell's Prophecy from The Apostle's Dialogue.

**

S IX OF THEM crossed the Division Bridge as a vanguard. Blaze at the head of the group, with Raven on his right, Skaa on his left and Sorrow, Flo, and Vervain bringing up the rear. The copseman had restated this wasn't his fight, but that the way they were going was also the way home. He wouldn't follow them into battle.

Smoke choked the air at ground level along the river bank. Displaced people lined the shore and their squalling children ran wild in the shallows. They'd come here to escape the flames that had already consumed their houses. Despite the odd explosion of marsh gases, this was the safest place they could think to go.

"Youkai!" The alarm rippled among their numbers, voices raised in fear. "Youkai! Youkai!" The chorus reminded Blaze of the chiming cathedral bells.

One brave fool charged towards them, a shotgun in hand.

"Turn back," he warned, his hand quaking so badly he was barely able to grip the gun. "If you don't, I'll render you into dust."

He fired into the air, sending the warning shot high over their heads. Screams rang out among the crowd. Then silence: painful, terrified silence, so palpable you could taste it alongside the ash in the air.

Blaze snatched the shotgun and threw it into the river. "Our gripe is with Talon, not you. Stand aside and none of you will be harmed."

Don't trust them... Come away... The whispers of those afeared impoverished people sallied through the air. One little girl screamed when Raven turned towards her.

"Shhh!" He raised his finger to his lips and she buried her face in her mother's skirts. The mother scowled and made the sign of the apostles. Strange how faith was magically restored whenever the bogeymen came to town.

Her actions were echoed amongst the crowd. Then with one purpose, the scores of refugees parted to allow them to pass.

Raven took point when they accessed the dank passageway into the cathedral that ran from quayside, Sorrow the rear, which left Blaze stuck in the middle like a spare part again. Flo and Skaa had headed in the front way, intent on causing a diversion. The copse-man had left when they'd turned from the copse road into the warehouse district muttering something about a contract he had to fulfil. Regardless, Blaze wished they'd all leave off trying to protect him and let him get to the part where he wrung Talon's scrawny neck.

Fact—he knew Talon had Asha because the moment before she'd slipped from his thoughts he'd seen the bastard through her own eyes, all blood-stained golden ringlets, manicured eyebrows, and sadistic smile. The fact that the bastard had dared to touch Asha raised Blaze's blood to boiling point. One barrel of salted fish exploded as he walked by, showering them all in scales and fragments of fins. If Talon had in any way hurt her—anymore than he already had—he was going to chop him into little bits and hand feed him to the grubs in the castle walls.

Actually, maybe the chopping part was a given.

A second barrel caught fire, and Sorrow shoved him forward before they were pelted with more fishy bits.

Blaze fingered the gun in his pocket. He had no intention of using it against Talon. A bullet wasn't likely to cause the rune-marked alchemist any more pain than a flea bite, but the feel of the polished metal beneath his fingertips offered a strange sort of comfort. Talon was going to look like a glorious piece of modern art once he'd reformed him a little. What he'd achieved with Grace and Florian had been the practice run. Talon would be the pièce de résistance.

So, a nice squishy shape, then chopping, then grubs. He had it all worked out.

Damn, this tunnel went on for miles.

Finally, a few paces ahead of him, Raven came to a halt in what was clearly an old garderobe. Blaze could just imagine the old bishop occupying the privy seat. Sadly, Talon wasn't using the facilities. He guessed it was too much to ask to catch him with his pants down.

"There's supposed to be a door," Blaze insisted, squinting at each of the walls in turn.

"Allow me." Sorrow shuffled up from behind. It only took a few seconds to locate the catch, but to Blaze it seemed like eternity. Seven minutes, maybe eight since he'd lost all sense of Asha, while they were locating the steps to the quayside storage room. The bond between them was too new to know whether she'd simply stepped out of range, or if something worse had happened.

Sorrow stepped first into the dimly lit room, releasing his sword from his scabbard as he moved. Blaze followed immediately on his heels. He caught a single glimpse of Asha before she simply vanished before his eyes, leaving him staring straight at Talon over the ridge of Sorrow's shoulder.

She'd been right there and yet he hadn't sensed her.

The alchemist gave him a devious smile, clutching to his chest a tear-shaped crystal. "Ah, the fire-starters have arrived."

Blaze lifted his arm to point, but Sorrow moved at the same time, forcing him to adjust his aim. The lectern on the far-side of the room burst into flames, while Sorrow's sword cleaved twice through Talon's image as if he were a mirage.

"I see your aim's not much improved," Talon cackled. "Do enjoy." His image shimmered and then fractured.

"Look left," yelled Raven from behind them. Talon now stood at the foot of the long acid scarred table that had recently been shoved out of position causing large scale destruction of the numerous chemical components it housed. Raven sent a knife flying in that direction, which Talon swept aside with a whispered command. The blade clattered harmlessly onto the floor amongst the spillages, where acid started eating into the blade.

Talon swept up two of the intact vials from the table and smashed them against the wainscoting, before making a particularly hasty retreat. The sickly sweet scent of almonds infused the air. Raven, who stood closest to the mingling, fizzing liquids immediately bent double and began coughing up whatever he'd eaten for lunch. "Get out," he warned, between heaves. "Don't let the bastard escape."

"Bugger, that's rank." Blaze clamped a hand across his face as he ran through the rapidly growing cloud of fumes being released by the effervescing liquids. Tears clouded his vision, and his lungs burned so badly he almost believed that if he looked down he'd find a chasm melted through his chest. Still, he managed to grab Raven's collar and haul him along in his wake as he swam through the gas, which was now thickening into strands that clung to the skin like spider's silk.

Of course, the bastard alchemist had locked the damn door.

Blaze beat his fist against the wood. It'd take too long to burn their way out, and it wasn't the sort of door that even the combined effort of three demons was likely to kick open.

"It's okay, I've got it." Sorrow muscled in alongside him and bent to the latch. In a deep soft voice he whistled a string of notes into the keyhole. Blaze's skin tingled as though a current had just been run through it. He couldn't quite catch the tune but there were words written into the notes and they seemed to curl around his senses, coaxing, caressing. It was reminiscent of the tingle that ran up his spine right before his wings came. More immediately disturbing, the wooden door suddenly acquired what he could only describe as sentience.

"Open," Sorrow commanded.

The door shuddered as if questioning Sorrow's authority, and then slowly swung open.

Blaze immediately dived through the gap.

"Be careful," Sorrow called after him.

Blaze glanced back and saw he was supporting Raven over the threshold. His chief guard appeared to have regained control of his guts but lost his sea legs.

"Blaze, wait. You don't want a war of words in the old tongue. Talon won't hold back."

He didn't want him to hold back. He wanted this over and done with. Outcome—one of them dead. Preferably Talon.

Mayhem lay ahead in the cloisters. The clash of steel mingled with the sound of gunfire and the bellowing of conflicting commands. Skaa and Florian had forced their way in through the main cathedral doors, and a group of Talon hunters now fanned around them. Talon stood on the central dais, his hand raised.

In horror Blaze watched as Talon opened a jagged crack in the fabric of the world that neatly sucked in the flames that had spread from the outer walls to the roof, before closing it again as if it had been invisibly zipped.

"Deranged fool." Sorrow and Raven caught up with him. "He's messing with things that have a habit of coming back to bite you on the arse. You don't just pop things out of existence. Everything ends up somewhere and you never know whose backyard you're going to dump your laundry on."

"Bastard's just showing off," Raven muttered. He remained a little green about the gills. "Let's give him something to worry about." He darted towards the dais. Blaze caught Sorrow's arm as he made to follow.

"Did you see what happened to Asha? She was there when we burst in. I saw her just for a moment."

The penetrating, yet almost quizzical look Sorrow gave him stopped him dead in his tracks. He knew what he'd seen. Asha had been there.

"I didn't see her. Sorry. It was dingy in there, and to be honest I was rather more focused upon what Talon was planning to do with the rock he was holding."

"What rock? You mean the crystal?"

"Crystals are used to make multi-dimensional prisons. Be wary of him throwing anything at you."

"No," he realised. "That's what he's done to Asha." It was the reason he couldn't properly sense her anymore. "How do we get her out?"

Sorrow shook him. "Blaze, you don't."

No, this couldn't be. He refused to let that sick bastard tear them apart again. "Asha," he yelled, charging straight for the dais and the bleached-white skin of Talon's form. He'd shake that gem loose and smash it into a thousand pieces. Only some vague recollection told him that wouldn't free her. She'd remain trapped in one of the fragments he created, perhaps in a sliver no wider than his fingernail.

Talon saw him coming, or rather he'd tracked Raven's approach and realised Blaze would be following. The alchemist scooted off his perch, an irrepressible grin stretched across his face.

Brows drawn, Blaze pumped his legs harder in his bid to reach Talon. Raven, who was much closer, shifted shape as he ran. His wings fanned from his back, prompting further shrieks of alarm from all the black-clad demon hunters in the room.

Raven ploughed straight through the line of warriors protecting their leader, knocking the pair who lay directly into his path over a low iron railing that bordered an ancient sculpture of a po-faced lady.

Raven took to the air, his black wings stretched wide as he hurtled straight towards Talon, only for his flight to be abruptly terminated as a dainty stone hand clasped him tight around the waist.

"Aw, shit!" Blaze skidded to a halt. Sorrow bumped into the back of him. Gargoyle was his first thought, but he wasn't entirely sure the stone creature bore more than passing resemblance to the pair he'd seen shattered into pieces on his audience chamber floor.

"Bastard's woken her," Sorrow growled into his ear. Talon had used the same trick Sorrow had demonstrated on the bedchamber door to coax the statue of—oh, who the hell knew who it was—from her gentle repose. The important point was that she'd woken angry. Her formerly beatific expression had transformed. She grinned and showed more teeth than any woman had a right to, and Blaze had seen enough razor sharp fangs recently to know exactly how many equated too many.

The statue cocked its marble head, so that its unblinking eyes stared straight at him.

"Hell! Now what do we do? She's huge."

Sorrow shook his head.

The former idol ran to a good twelve feet in height and bore the musculature of a champion gymnast. It was perfectly clear she also possessed the strength and passion to rip off heads, chew diamonds, and generally be a royal pain in the arse.

Skaa and Florian managed to fight their way through to them. They kept up their momentum and hacked straight at her ankles.

"Put him down," Blaze yelled, trying to draw the bitch's attentions so she didn't simply step on the bugs at her feet.

It worked, sort of, but not before she'd taken a bite out of Raven's middle. Damn bitch spat it out as if it were foul, and then dropped him.

Blaze tracked every inch of Raven's descent, following both his body and the column of Blood Rain that hung in the air behind him. He ran, oblivious to all around him, staggered under the impact, collapsing to his knees with Raven held fast within his arms.

His friend blinked at him and groaned.

"You're a heavy bugger to keep catching."

"What's everybody got against my belly?"

Blaze looked down at the wound. It was nasty but not nearly as deep or grotesque as he'd anticipated. He didn't think about it. He bit into his own wrist and fed Raven the blood. Only as the wound began to heal did he realise much of the noise around him had quieted, and that no one had approached trying to end their lives. A full third of Talon's demon hunters stood with their noses strained into the air as if they could snort Raven's blood right out of the sky.

The world had gone damn raving mad. It needed straightening out, and fast.

Skaa pulled a crystal globe out from beneath his robes and sent it hurtling towards the statue's head. Rather than shattering, the ball stopped inches before her face. It flashed brilliant white, prompting a howl of outrage. She flailed blindly at the sphere, but the light ball dodged repeatedly out of reach. It began making an increasingly high pitched whine.

"I hope that's not a signal to call in the troops," Blaze growled. He still didn't want the youkai in the City.

"Good call." Sorrow slapped his brother across the back.

"Momentary distraction, that's all. It won't keep her busy for more than a minute or two." Skaa shrugged off the praise, already on the move again and unravelling a rope from beneath his swaddling black clothes. "You go left, and I'll take the right." He thrust one end of the cord into Sorrow's hands, and they began to circle the statue.

"No!" Blaze yelled after them. Not that he objected to hogtieing the bitch, but Skaa had hammered home the point of this. It was a distraction. While they were pansying about maypole dancing with a lump of marble, Talon was laughing his bloody socks off.

The statue finally hit the hovering globe causing it to smash. She made an ineffectual grab for the brothers, who merrily skipped out of her way as they pulled the rope tight around her calves.

"What we need is a ruddy great chisel," he heard one of them say.

Damn demons were enjoying this.

He shook off Raven's hold upon his wrist.

Blaze scanned the room for signs of Talon. Somehow he knew the alchemist wouldn't have gone far. He caught sight of him in the choir stalls. Blaze summoned all the rage in his soul— rather a lot—and set a ball of pure energy hurtling in Talon's direction. He wanted Asha back. No way was that bastard keeping her from him.

The impact sent a fan of sparks right up Talon's back.

The hit gave Blaze the warm fuzzies.

"Yes!" He pounded the air, and then broke into a sprint. He headed straight for the alchemist as he readied another energy bolt.

"We need to get this bastard fast." Raven fell in beside him. Blaze didn't bother to reply. He already had Talon in his sights. Sadly, although the second fiery bolt hit the target, Talon emerged unscathed with not so much as a soot mark staining his skin. He soared upwards on snowy wings.

"No. Not again." Memories of Talon fleeing the warehouse overlaid his current flight. This time he wasn't letting Talon escape. The glint of a jewel in Talon's palm spurred him to greater effort.

Blaze ran through the agony of shifting forms. He lost his T-shirt in the process, although not his jacket. The black rags fell away as his wings flapped propelling him up towards the cruck roof.

Raven stayed with him. That bite had to have hurt, and the wound hadn't fully closed judging by the streamers of coppery dust Raven continued to paint through the air. Still, he was sticking to his vow to cover Blaze's back.

Talon landed on the upper storey of the cloisters, where he slid between the columns of the balustrade and disappeared from sight amongst the shadows of the walkway.

Blaze landed a yard or two away and hopped through a similar gap. "Cut him off," he yelled at Raven, who immediately kicked up his flight speed and swept to a landing at the opposite end of the balcony. They had Talon now. It was just a matter of pinning him down, clawing the crystal out of his hand and using some good old fashion persuasion techniques to ensure his cooperation in releasing Asha.

The building beneath him shook as he sprinted after the alchemist. Below, on the ground floor of the transept Skaa and Sorrow had felled the statue. Through the gaps in the stone railing Blaze saw them clamber over the living marble onto its shoulders and start hacking at the back of its neck.

Ahead of him on the balcony, Talon came to a sudden stop. He looked back and forth between Blaze and Raven knowing he was trapped.

Flames coiled in blue and orange tendrils around Blaze's clenched fist. They might temporarily knock him off balance, but he knew it wasn't enough to take the bastard out. It had been a mistake to display his rage back in the warehouse. Talon had done what any sensible soul would do. He'd ward-marked his body against the magical fire.

Talon smiled at them both, then opened another crack in the ether. Only this time he cut through the solid rock of the cathedral wall to carve a path onto the roof. A fraction ahead, Raven dived through the newly formed door with Blaze on his heels. He crumpled immediately as he the cool air hit his body, forcing Blaze to pull up sharp to avoid tumbling over him and right off the roof.

He caught Raven around the waist. Blood coated the front of his clothing and covered Blaze's hands. He knew the bite wound was still bleeding but... this was more than that. Talon appeared right before them. A long slender knife glinted in the moonlight, the ruby glow along its silvered length more than just the reflection of the crimson moon.

"Forgive me, but all this chasing about is growing tiresome, and it was necessary to even the odds."

"You fucking bastard." Raven seemed to grow

impossibly heavy within Blaze's arms. He felt his friend slipping and gripped him tighter. The roof dipped then rose again at this point on the building, but if he released him, Raven would still roll into the dip where the gutters ran.

"Give me, Asha," Blaze growled.

Talon smiled sadistically, and turned the crystal prison between his fingers. It was a clear white diamond, cut like a teardrop, but with what appeared to be a speck of coal locked in the centre. Asha, he realised, panicked by the glimpse of her.

Flames lit like those on a gas ring in every rain channel along the roof.

"Temper, temper," Talon taunted. "Tell me what's she's worth, Blaze. The life of your friend, perhaps?" The evil bastard punched Raven, who groaned, at least proving he was still alive. "She's mine. I raised her to be perfect. Why would I let her go to a foolish half-breed who can barely remember his own name?"

"She doesn't love you."

"She doesn't need to. This has never been about love." He lashed out again, aiming for Raven's face. Blaze weathered the impact, clinging to his friend, determined to hold onto him and not to let him fade away or burn. Fresh blood poured from Raven's nostrils.

"You're wrong, Talon." It had always been about love. His love of the City and its crazy inhabitants, and his pursuit of someone to care for him, and to care about. He hadn't specifically sought Asha at the start of this mayhem, but he'd found her. The one woman who could make him whole.

He made a mad grab for the diamond.

Talon easily dodged. Then he darted forward again, coming in close enough for Blaze to feel his breath, as he stabbed down into Raven's gut.

"No."

Raven's scream pieced his eardrums.

"Raven?" Blood spurted from the wound, and rapidly began to powder. Blaze sagged to his knees beneath the weight of his friend.

"Another move like that and I'll slice his throat from ear to ear. He might tolerate a little blood loss without going all ruby snowflake on us but I think you'll find demons choke just as readily as anyone else." Talon took a step backwards as he spoke. "Now Blaze, not so much as a blink." He continued to back away, and after six or seven paces, turned his back on them and fled.

"Coward. Fine, run then. I'll catch you."

"I count on it, demon prince."

Blaze watched Talon's skinny form retreating along the roof, with tears of frustration filling his eyes. He needed Asha, but he couldn't let Raven go. He clung to the demon sprawled across his lap, listened in horror at the wheezy rattle of his chest, while he pressed down on the wound. Blood still oozed from the stab wounds and coated his hands. Blood Rain hung over their heads like a cloud.

"You'll be all right, my friend. It'll be all right." He heard himself say it, but to hell if he believed it. Pain wracked his body just from remaining still. He was losing Asha. Talon had taken her. And Raven was slipping away from him too.

He couldn't face either outcome.

His pulse pounded against the side of his skull. Then his vision turned red.

"Blayzzzzz." Raven coughed up a well of blood. He feebly tried to raise a hand, seeking Blaze's wrist.

He ought to let him suckle. He could restore him that way, but if they remained here long enough to mend the wounds there'd be no chance of ever catching Talon. And looking down through the crimson veil of his vision, he wasn't sure that he could even give enough blood to make Raven heal.

"Blaze?" Sorrow barrelled through the newly opened door in the stonework. "Talon?" he asked, immediately squatting down by their sides. He took one look at Raven and another at Blaze. "Go." He took Raven's weight in his arms. "I can get him stable enough to haul his arse home. Asha I can't help you with."

Paralysis held Blaze for a moment. Then he leaned in and kissed goodbye Raven's blood-ringed lips. "Stay strong." He squeezed his bodyguard's fingertips.

"Go," Sorrow ordered.

Blaze was already running. He pounded across the tiles as far as the weathervane and then slipped unsteadily down the sloping roof into the drainage channel that was still awash with lilac flames. Staying clear of the fire he'd started, he followed the channel several metres before clawing his way up again towards the apex of the roof over the cathedral nave.

Talon stood balanced on the very edge of the roof, his back to Blaze, facing the plaza. His snowy wings seemed especially bright against the backdrop of the Blood Moon. All around them the sky was coloured mustard yellow. Flakes of ash danced on the breeze like flakes of falling snow.

Precariously balanced and immeasurably grateful for the gift of wings, Blaze edged along the apex towards Talon's perch. Only when he was within five feet of Talon did the alchemist turn.

Talon's wings folded around him and he formed a silhouette against the fat rosy circle of the moon. He looked impossibly fragile, and perversely angelic standing there. His skin bleached bone white. Dark circles shadowed his eyes, the irises burned cerulean blue.

"There's no need to run anymore. It's just us now. No more interruptions. No more hangers-on." Even as he spoke the cannons on the plaza blasted more alchemical grapeshot into the air. Flashes of energy scorched the sides of the building, sending showers of orange and lilac high into the night sky. The stained glass portraits of the silent, abandoned saints splintered sending glittering shards into the air.

"Should I mourn the loss of my home?"

"Mourn the loss of life," Blaze replied. The moonlight caught the silver tracery of the ward marks burned into Talon's skin as he lifted his arm to smooth his hair back off his face. On his inner wrist the Blood Moon shone with a pinkish blush.

"Just whose actions have threatened the most lives?" Talon countered. He dismissed Blaze's reply with a tick of his head. "I weeded out the psychopaths; either employed them or executed them. You've burned the commoners from their homes. Are your demons going to feed and clothe them, help re-build their lives brick by brick? What support are you going to provide, Prince of the Youkai? There'll be none forthcoming from the Heights."

He laughed.

"Prince of a drab wasteland is what you'll be. Look around you. Does it warm the depths of that old soul of yours to see all that you've accomplished?"

Talon squatted giving Blaze a clear panoramic view of the Old City. It was all laid out before him like a child's model. Ash swirled in the breeze and clung to the roof tiles, through which specks of red slate peeked like coppery spots of blood. To the left the Birdcage was alight. The entirety of the Eyrie lit up like a warning beacon. Screams and the clash of arms filled the streets below and fireworks sparked off the sides of the cathedral.

The people had found the cannons and turned them on one another, while screaming that the youkai were among them and that they had to be found. He watched a man hit by one of the glass orbs freeze and then fracture into a million tiny shards of ice.

So much wasted life.

He'd done this. This destruction was his responsibility.

In dismay Blaze looked down at his hands, they were copper stained and soiled with the residue of Raven's blood. "I never wanted this," he muttered, only deep down he knew that fifty years ago at least part of him had. He'd plotted and planned events that would bring them to this point. If only he could rewind time and truly know what had been in his heart and mind when he'd initiated his own rebirth.

Had it been an act of desperation from one who had lived too long to wish to still go on, or had he craved the crown he now bore?

Talon raised his arms and dragged forked lightning from the sky, which he threw at Blaze. The blue streamer ran along the apex of the roof and into Blaze. It surged up his spine, overfilling him with energy, and snatching his vision from him.

For a moment he thought it would all end. Even welcomed that prospect. Then he remembered his friends.

"Asha," he called, blindly stretching out his arms. "Asha."

Of course, she didn't take his hand, prompting him to utter a second word. "Burn."

"Because that's really going to work." Talon continued to laugh. "I think we've already established that I've warded my arse against your poxy theatrics."

Blaze maintained his focus. Why argue with the deluded? Besides, having Talon talk actually helped with his targeting. He sought the silence where Asha should have been. The tiny void of emotion.

The summoned flames ripped down his arms and out through his fingers, straight at the vessel in which she lay trapped.

Strike one. Talon dropped the gem which skittered away to land in the gutter.

Strike two, he dived and snatched the key from around Talon's throat, which curiously seemed to even out the odds.

"You'll return that," Talon bellowed. He was bleached white in Blaze's dying vision, except for the pinpoints of blue fire that were his eyes. "You'll return it at once."

"Something important?" Blaze taunted. He tentatively back-stepped along the roof, taking care with his footing. "Free Asha and I'll give you your precious key." He prayed Talon didn't realise his sight was nearly gone.

"Why should I trust you, demon?"

"Seems to me you don't have any choice. Free her."

"Tap the key to the rock, and then toss it back or I'll not give you the command to free her."

Shit! He'd have to slide down into the gutter and risk sailing off the side of the cathedral into the tide of flames and smoke licking at the walls. So not good with his flat, monotone vision.

But then what was the point of wings if he didn't use them?

Blaze flexed and rose. He noticed Talon's eyes narrow. Realised he'd moved, but couldn't see what he had thrown. The long poniard struck his shoulder, but failed to pierce the leather plate.

Treacherous bastard was already attempting to renege on their deal.

The tiles were slippery near the edge. Blaze had to cling fast to the iron gutter and keep his wings in motion just to maintain his perch. He sloshed his hand about in the river of stagnant milky rain water, and pulled out clumps of moss and chips of broken roof tiles.

Asha. He had to have her. She was part of him now.

Finally, his hand closed around the tear-shaped diamond. He couldn't see it at all, not even when he held it right in front of his nose, but he could feel the facets of it, and knew this was the one.

He tapped.

Nothing changed.

"The key, demon." Talon's demand rang shrilly in his ears.

"Say the words. Free her first." Oh, Lord, damnit! He threw the key, and heard it ping against the tiles. He didn't know if Talon stooped or flew to retrieve it, because Asha blinked back into existence right before his eyes, and the sight of her ghostly outline sent a chill through his entire body. Blaze stared at her with his flat white vision trying to determine if she was as insubstantial as she seemed, or whether she was as solid as he.

Had Talon kept his word? He wasn't sure. Maybe his beloved Asha had simply found her way out of the maze.

Her fingers briefly traced the curve of his cheek. Then her lips drew back revealing elongated fangs.

"He's mine," she snarled.

Asha left him precariously balanced and effortlessly danced over the rooftop, light as feather, and agile as the breeze. When she reached Talon she pushed her palms into the thick of his snow-white feathers. His eyes widened in shock.

"What are you..." His words transformed into a scream of unfamiliar syllables. Blaze sensed the air molecules around him sit up and pay attention, but the sentence was never finished.

Asha sank her teeth deep into the side of Talon's throat.

He struggled a bit at first, but she raked her hands through his feathers and slowly he stilled. His face filled up with bliss.

Talon's eyelids drooped, all the fight gone from his limbs. Asha released him, and he slumped, and then rolled. He fell past Blaze, over the gutter, and dropped into the light of the flames caressing the building, becoming a moving white blur against a whiter background.

Over. He'd never believed it would end.

The hem of Asha's skirt brushed his knee and Blaze realised his vision was slowly returning. There were slices of grey bleeding into the white landscape alongside dots of yellow and streaks of green. He listened to her purge the blood she'd just drunk from her body. By the time she'd wiped the spittle from her lips he could see shades of red again.

"I don't want him to be part of us," she said by way of explanation.

Blaze shook his head. "He never was. He's just a hellish nuisance."

Asha tugged him back onto his feet, and he rested against the steep slope of the roof. "What now?" she asked.

"Home." There were Raven's wounds to heal and other problems to face. Right now, though, he wanted peace enough to cradle Asha in his arms and to appreciate the many joys he had in his life. He remained carefully balanced a moment or two, content simply to feel the rise and fall of her breasts where her bodice pressed tight to his torso.

"I think it's going to rain."

"You?" she asked as the first spots of drizzle trickled over their upturned faces.

Blaze shook his head. "Just a timely deluge."

He swept Asha up into his arms and with her cradled firmly to his chest, he dived off the roof and soared high into the air making for their castle in the sky.

11: FALLEN ANGEL

TALON CRASHED THROUGH the roof of a fire damaged house on Weymark Street. If he'd possessed the strength he'd have cursed Blaze for every scratch, every bruise and scrape that marked his body. For a long time he lay in the dark staring up through the hole through which he'd fallen, gazing at the distant stars and reliving the moment of pure ecstasy when Asha's fists had closed around his feathers and her fangs had pierced his neck.

He still wondered if the spark of life that remained in his body was enough to sustain him.

Come morning, he still remained, though he was anaemic and horribly parched.

The sun rose and light bleached the glow of the runes that marked his skin. Only then did the real pain kick in. One wing had broken completely in the fall. Now, the weight of crushed feathers and bone made it virtually impossible to rise.

He had no idea how to set a wing, assuming such a thing were even possible to do for yourself. The only plus side, was that all the fruitless wing manipulation taught him a valuable lesson about thresholds. A little feather stroking made everything tolerable and went a long way to alleviate the pain, whereas over much made it wrack like a hot poker from hell.

Not nearly enough blood flowed around his body, only enough to keep his heart pumping. If said heart had been inside his body, he'd have been truly doomed. Luckily the half-pickled remains of the organ that had once beat inside his chest currently resided in a far safer location. As long as it continued to beat there, he couldn't truly die, much as part of him wished ardently for death at this moment.

Talon wriggled on his belly across the charred and broken attic boards to hide from the sunlight. His only consolation was that despite a few hiccups, phase one of his plan was now complete. He'd opened the pathway to hell, and with the youkai running rampant through the Old City, the moguls in the Heights would finally find themselves ready to listen.

He spent the day dwelling on the subject, while huddled in the shadows listening to the house timbers creak. At nightfall, he caught a rat and ate it whole. It gave him enough energy for a simple spell. Talon wove the inscription into the air, and the magic lifted him from the hovel to a glass penthouse in the Heights.

"Remove the wing," he told the startled doctor whose house party he'd just crashed. "It's fucked, and may well re-grow."

ABOUT THE AUTHOR

MADELYNNE IS A New York Times & USA Today bestselling author. She wrote her first novel after discovering Black Lace Books in the 1990s. After escaping the Hotel California, she dived into storytelling full time. Her books are filled with bisexual bad boys who like to get down and dirty, and stories so angst-filled you know they're going to hurt.

She lives in the UK near the Welsh border, where you can find her surrounded by books, drinking rapidly cooling decaf coffee, and listening to loud music.

Come hang out with her via her newsletter, where she shares what she's reading, watching, listening to, and snippets about her current projects.